The White Light Chronicles:

OBSIDIAN WHITE— SHADES OF VIOLET

R J TRUMAN

Copyright © 2013 R J Truman
All rights reserved.

ISBN: 1481147404
ISBN-13: 9781481147408

Library of Congress Control Number: 2012922945
CreateSpace Independent Publishing Platform
North Charleston, South Carolina

Prologue

Meet the Whites

Lucy was a quiet girl who always kept herself to herself and never caused trouble. At least that's what her school reports always said. She was also an elf she just didn't know it. That bit wasn't in her reports either.

She had always been aware that she was different from the other girls in her class, but she could never work out why. Her family had always lived in the same village, as far as she knew. Well they had lived there all her life anyway, they hadn't moved from some far flung corner of the planet or been beamed down from space, as far as she knew.

She couldn't work out why she wasn't like everyone else. If her parents had told her, it would have explained a lot. Like why she didn't fit in. She was different with her golden sand coloured skin and red hair. All her parents wanted was for her to live a normal life, they wanted to fit in and not draw attention to themselves, which given their appearance was impossible. Little did they know that their need to live a 'normal life' would create one big abnormal problem.

As for her family they lived in a reasonably sized house, situated at the edge of a forest on the outskirts of the village of New Haven. A long track wound its way up to the house and there were fields on either side of it.

The fields were owned by Lucy's father, and even though they were perfect farmland he never farmed them. The local farmers all thought he was mad, because he had the best fields for miles. When he was once asked why he never farmed them, he simply replied that the ground had a greater purpose, and would say no more. This only helped to fuel the rumours in the village that Mr. White was totally unhinged, and generally mad.

Lucy's father like Lucy, kept himself very much to himself, and rarely ever left the house; like Lucy's mother he had eyes the colour of the leaves in autumn, but unlike hers his were turning brown around the edges. His hair also seemed to have turn browner with the years, like the leaves on a deciduous tree before they die and fall to the ground.

Lucy's mother's hair was a warm orange that grandly turned to a vivid red at the tips, and she didn't look a day older than Lucy. Unlike Lucy and her father, she took a more active roll in the community; she even joined the local women's club. The other women in the club were very jealous of her exotic tasting jams. One thing Lucy and her mother had in common was their golden sand coloured skin. Her father's skin was more a pale sun bleached sandy colour.

Curious to know more about her background. Lucy often went exploring in the loft. Most of the time it proved pointless, however once she found an old photo of her parents in which they had green eyes, and what looked to Lucy like dark green hair. Both parents insisted that something must have happened to the photo when it was developed. Nothing was said about the photo again although Lucy often wondered about it. She wanted to take it to school to show the photography teacher and ask what could have happened to it however, much to Lucy's annoyance it soon went missing. Not at all suspicious, really.

One Night in New Heaven

So setting the scene it was Halloween, and as usual the teenagers of the village were having their annual Halloween party in, surprise! Yes the village hall. Lucy had the sudden urge to go, but she couldn't figure out why. She had never in all her years ever wanted to go before. For one thing everyone at the school she attended hated her, and for another, Halloween was especially awful, as they would all joke that with her bizarre appearance she wouldn't need a costume. Jokes aside all she knew was she had to go. Something deep inside her was telling that this was what she had to do. It was like she felt compelled to have to do it.

Her mother was thrilled; she finally got to help Lucy get ready to go out. She decided that Lucy should wear a jet black witch's wig; a short black dress, and spiders web tights. She covered Lucy's skin in white body paint, lined her eyes with kohl, and applied tons of black mascara to her red lashes; finally she painted her lips blood red. However, she needn't have bothered going to all that effort, as Lucy never made it to the party. In fact, she didn't make it very far at all.

Lucy was walking down the dark, narrow, winding lane that ran from her house towards the direction of the village when something in one of her father's fields caught her attention. The fields were always so empty, apart from the obvious grass, and the occasional tree, there was nothing untoward to be seen in the fields, until now. One of the fields was full of rainbow coloured tepees. In the centre of the field, surrounded by the other rainbow coloured tepees stood a dark purple tepee. It was larger than the others and had a strange flag attached to it that appeared to be moving as if in a light breeze, but Lucy couldn't help but notice that the air was still. Not a single leaf rustled, or blade of grass stirred, yet still the flag danced on. She couldn't make out what was on the flag, not that she cared. She was more intrigued by that fact that it was moving! When all her senses told her this was not possible. The flag moved like a snake slithering through the sky,

There was something else that seemed to draw Lucy in, there was a light aroma in the air that seemed strange yet alluring. She couldn't figure out all of the smells, many were new to her, they were intriguing. She liked them, she knew that much and felt the strong need to get closer to the source of them. Above all else Lucy found herself strongly drawn to the purple tepee, so much so that she climbed over a gate hidden by brambles in the hedge, catching her dress as she did so. She didn't mind; she pulled the fabric and waited for it to rip before flinging her legs over the top of the gate. She didn't care about the stinging nettles that she very gracefully landed in. All she could think about was getting to the tepee and as she walked closer towards it was then she noticed him. He was tall with long dark blue almost black hair, which matched the colour of the night sky. His skin was paler than the moon and his eyes although they were as black as coal sparkled like the stars. He held a pewter goblet shaped like a dragon in his hand. Its tail was the stem of the goblet, and in its wings was cupped a glass. The glass was pure obsidian and contained a dark violet liquid.

"Drink" was the only word that Lucy could remember coming from his lips. Somehow they wrapped themselves around her head and enchanted her mind. She drained the glass dry. Everything after that seemed like a dark dream, not quite a nightmare but not a pleasant dream either. They entered the tepee, and they kissed. She remembered that much without trouble. But after that it was pain mixed with a feeling she had never felt before.

And So It Begins
A Lake in the Forest of Dreams

Obsidian stirred and slowly stretched out her soft golden- sand tinted leg. She tried very carefully not to wake Torch the goat- sized dragon sleeping at the foot of her bed. She owned Torch ever since she was only a few days old, and the dragon had looked after her for the seventeen years that had followed. Torch had an awful temper when she was woken up. Often when disturbed from her sleep she would set alight objects in Obsidian's room. Over the years Obsidian had replaced several sets of curtains, and even an entire bookshelf. Rowena Obsidian's tutor, would often go off for days at a time trying to replace Obsidian's burned possessions. Despite the fact that Torch had an awful temper, in a strange way Obsidian felt attached to the temperamental dragon. Who unknown to Obsidian had remained in her shell for thousands of years and only hatched when

Obsidian was born. When she was only a few hours old she flew from her nest, and in through Obsidian's window, snuggled up next to her in her cot, and made herself quite at home. Torch watched over Obsidian ever since that day, knowing in her heart she had to protect Obsidian from whatever dangers life could send her way.

"Obsidian!!!!!!!!!!!!!, It's time for your archery lesson" yelled Rowena from outside Obsidian's window. She had done this every day since Obsidian was three. It might seem extreme to teach a three year old such things. However Obsidian wasn't your average three- year- old. Even now she wasn't your average teenager.

Right on cue Torch jumped up from the bed letting a jet of pink flames spray out of her nostrils. Obsidian dodged the flames and made her way out of the room. This was after she had rescued some clothes from a slightly singed wardrobe. Torch came bumbling along after her.

Although Obsidian enjoyed her archery lessons, and other what she deemed as pointless fighting skills lessons, her preferred activity was to read books about far off places and strange lands, these were really just books Rowena brought in about the outside world. The everyday world that you and I live in. She also spent lots of time with Torch, running around the forest and chasing its various inhabitants. Occasionally she would chase Rowena, who hated this as she was much slower than Obsidian, and always got caught. Despite her slowness, she still ran much faster than you or I could ever possibly dream of running. With that in mind try to think of how fast Obsidian must be.

Now for her home, Obsidian lived in an Elizabethan style manor house situated in the middle of the most bizarre yet amazing forest you could imagine. She shared the house and its grounds with her grandmother and her mother. Her grandfather had 'died,' or so she believed, on the very same day that she was born. In reality her grandfather was still technically alive, he just no longer alive on Earth. He had returned to his homeland, which will become apparent later in this story, or maybe even in another story altogether. You'll just have to wait and see. Her mother was always lost in a daydream and of no use to her. As for her grandmother, she was always far too busy with important, grown-up things. She never really had time for Obsidian. Most of the time it seemed to her like no one could be bothered with her, or really knew what to do with her.

The forest the house was situated in was at this time home to pixies, fairies, unicorns, and fauns among other creatures. It was the lake however that was the most beautiful thing in the whole of the forest. It was in a clearing a few hundred meters or so from the house. Each droplet of water in its vast depths was a water nymph; they were the most mesmerising creatures you could ever hope to see.

They would rise up out of the water like beautiful naked women made completely out of water. Unfortunately for them they could only rise a few meters above the surface of the water before they would burst like bubbles and shower down on the lake. It was an extraordinary sight to witness such a thing, and Obsidian never got tired of watching them. When each one burst they caught the light like water droplets and sent rainbows darting off all over the surface of the lake. It looked quite spectacular.

The lake was also teaming with mermaids. They would tease the nymphs by jumping up out of the water, and do back flips, somersaulting high above the surface of the water. Much higher than the nymphs could go. Often they would try to copy the mermaids but the nymphs would pop before they had the chance to do so much as one back flip. Sometimes the mermaids would pop the nymphs just for fun. Mostly, however, they would tend to just sit on the banks of the lake and laze around in the sun.

Right in the centre of the lake there was a boat, well you or me would recognise it as a canal barge. It was painted green and covered in ornate pictures of flowers. The beautifully painted barge was home to Gaia, or Mother Earth, as she is more commonly known. She had hair that hung around her head like clouds, and when it touched her dress of lush green grass it turned into a flowing river. Her skin looked like is was made of a deep dark red clay, her features

were soft and friendly, with eyes that were a wa
brown, and her teeth were gleaming white a
When she spoke it was a like a light whispering breeze, but when she was angry it would boom out of her like roaring treacherous thunder. Her abdomen seemed swollen for she forever looked pregnant, but as far as Obsidian knew she had no children. Little did she know that all the creations in the forest were Mother Earth's children. For at one time or another she had created them all, and for little reason other than that she could, and mostly because she got bored of well looking after the world as a whole.

A Brief History of Well, Everything

Obsidian felt worn out and achy after her three-hour archery lesson with Rowena, a tree nymph who despite her name spent most of her life as a willow tree that took up residence on the bank by the lake. She hated the fact that her name seemed to limit her to one form when she was capable of becoming so many. Well so many different tree forms that was. In her human form she most closely resembled the willow tree as she was thin and elegant, although regardless of her seeming elegance she often wore her hair in blonde dreadlocks. Rowena tried hard to get on with Obsidian, after all she was the one Gaia had chosen to train her. However she found her to be immature, and full of anger. She had so much potential, but lacked the discipline, and self-control she needed to be a truly great warrior.

Despite Obsidian's exhaustion, Rowena wasn't done with her. "Well now it's time for your first and well last history lesson"

Obsidian turned to Rowena with a face distorted by confusion.

"History? But why would I want to learn that? What use is that going to be? Obsidian could often be very sarcastic, and sometimes just plain rude. She had yet to learn any real manners, and Rowena was certain that it was not her place to teach her. Instead she fired back at her in a way that only made Obsidian worse.

"Use? Well, I'm glad I'm not teaching you. Really you have no idea do you? Well follow me to the lake" Once again Rowena was losing her patience with her downright stubborn student.

"To the lake? Who's going to teach me at the lake? The mermaids? Hmmm, or the water things? Um I don't think so"

She turned to walk back to the house, when Rowena grabbed her arm and marched her to the lake. When they reached the lake Rowena stopped, and Obsidian stumbled to a stop at her side.

"You're forgetting the one other person who lives on the lake" Rowena gestured toward the barge.

"Gaia?"

As if summoned, Gaia appeared on the deck of the barge.

"Come aboard and I'll tell you everything I know" Her voice was like a whisper in the wind.

"And she knows a lot, ha ha ha" giggled one of the mermaids as she swam past.

"Ok well that's all well and good, but I don't really want to take a whole lesson here on the bank, but as no one has taken the time to teach me how to swim, and not that I've ever checked, but I'm pretty sure I can't walk on water. How am I meant to get to that boat thing there?" As Obsidian spoke, her words oozed sarcasm and she pointed dismissively at the barge.

Just then the water on the lake began to ripple, and then the water nymphs rose up out of the lake. They parted to create a walkway and lined up like columns to clear the way for Obsidian shimmering in the sunlight and sending out thousands of tiny rainbows across the forest. Meanwhile the mermaids sat on the bank looking bored and somewhat unimpressed with the show the nymphs were providing.

Obsidian stepped forward and rather nervously walked through the nymphs to the barge. With every step she took the nymphs behind her came crashing down in great waves, returning to droplets of water. Once she reached the barge the mermaids had retuned to the water and started to put on a little show of their own. They did not like to think they could possibly be outdone by a load of bubble people.

"So you have come for your history lesson. Well, take a seat." She absent mindedly waved her hand in the direction of an ornately painted chair. It looked pretty enough, but was back breakingly uncomfortable. As Gaia spoke Obsidian felt a cold chill creep down her back. She had a feeling she wasn't going to be keen on history. Well, not the history she was about to hear anyway.

"Well where to start? Hmm, I guess I should start with the creation. Yes, I'll start there.

When the Almighty Power created the world, I came in to being to govern it, if you will. But I was not the only thing that was created; people were created too. They could roam around freely doing as they wished.

"Earth however was not the only place the Almighty Power created. He made the 'Higher Earth' a place where the souls of people go when they well, um, die. In the Higher Earth there were elves, and they were full of love and compassion. And so all was well and good for a while.

Well let's just say that one elf didn't want to play by the rules, he liked to torment the souls that came to the Higher Earth. He was wicked and cruel and evil, and all the things the Almighty One tried so hard to keep out of existence. But humans were also turning to violence. Wars were breaking out and murders were happening, and (seemed to be going wrong."

"That's when the Almighty Power created the Under World, and Lucifer was created to be the ruler of it. The first thing sent there was the naughty elf. Elves were made to represent the cycle of nature and change over time like a tree through the seasons to show people that nothing lasts forever, and that they should treasure their lives and all of the Almighty One's creations."

"But this design didn't fit in the Under World, so Lucifer went to work and created a creature worthy of his domain. This creature was tall with long dark blue, almost black hair, which matched the of the night sky. His skin was paler than the moon and his eyes although they were as black as coal sparkled like the stars. He was the first vampire. He liked to tease and torment the elf sent to the Under World, for although the elf was evil, the vampire was capable of much more. He could feed on the souls sent to the Under World by sucking the energy out of them, using it fuel his own body.

"Many more vampires were created, some male, some female. Their purpose was to inflict pain and torture on those evil souls sent to the Under World. But there was one vampire, the original one, who wanted more. He grew tired of dealing with the souls of the dead. He wanted to play with humans and feed from them. Somehow he tricked his way out of the Under World and found his way to Earth. No ones for sure how he managed to slip past Lucifer and escape, for Lucifer would never say. Hmmm wounded pride I'm sure.

"Well when he got to Earth, he found that he could feast on the blood of humans and in doing so turn them into vampires. Soon the vampires overran the lands and almost outnumbered the humans. That's when the Almighty sent down the rest of the elves for some elves lived here already, trying to teach humans the ways of peace. They did this subtly so not to make their true presence known to the humans. Your grandparents were the first elves sent down, anyway back to the point. They set up communities in which they could protect the humans with their great strength and magical powers. They set up a force field if you will around the human towns and cities that the vampires could not penetrate. They were far stronger than the vampires, and they were not driven by the primal instinct to hunt and kill and feed.

"The force fields worked for a time, but the design of the elves let them down, and like the leaves of the trees the elves withered, lost a lot of their power and so passed back to the Higher Earth. Leaving us with the situation we are in now where the vampires roam freely, with no one able to stop or control them. Humans don't fully understand what they really are, and, fueled by their need to be the best, strive to join with them."

Information Overload

Obsidian rose from her chair, and walked slowly to the side of the barge. Her head was down, and her face was a mix of confusion and frustration. She turned to Gaia raised her head, saying softly but clearly.

"I still don't see what all this has to do with me I mean really what do you want me to do about this? What can I do?" She had none of her normal sarcastic tone. She seemed for once to show genuine concern. Really she was worried about herself, and what was coming next.

Gaia smiled and motioned to Rowena to join them. With one great leap Rowena made her way from the shore to the barge. She made it look so easy, and Obsidian kicked herself that she hadn't thought to do such a thing. She was so annoyed at herself that she almost didn't notice that Gaia had infact started to talk again.

"I have a plan. Well, it is not totally my plan, but anyway here it goes. You and Rowena must leave the forest. Rowena has a place to stay in a city called Georgiana not so far from here you will go there. While you are there you will try your best to fit in with the locals, both human and vampire. And your task is to locate the whereabouts of your father. It won't be easy he goes by many names, as do we all. Once you find him, you must kill him. Well I say kill him, strictly speaking your father cannot die as such. But if you destroy his physical body his soul will be forced to return to the Under World. This is how I believe it works, I may be wrong. Let's hope for all of our sakes that I am not, Gaia's voice seemed heavy with doubt, and it was hard for even her to hide it.

"Right, so you want me to walk in to some city, whatever one of those happens to be, find my father, when I have no idea who he is and kill him? And are you going to tell me why me of all people has to do this?" Obsidian was back to her self again. She was so angry. Even after Gaia's somewhat epic speech she still felt she lacked all the information she needed.

"When he dies, so to speak, so will all of the creatures he has created. A part of him lives in them, in their blood; so when he dies, he will take that with him to the Under

World, and his creations will be free again or so I believe. Although I have heard other theories. Either way when he dies so do all the other vampires, His energy keeps them all alive." Once again Gaia didn't seem certain. She wished that she had taken more time to think this through and go over the facts. Then on the other hand this wasn't really her fight. Her main concern was the well-being of the world as a whole, regardless of whether it was infested with humans, vampires, or both, she only cared that they didn't hurt her precious Earth. Humans had done lots of damage, that much was true. Some cared though. No vampires cared. That, she told herself, was reason enough to side with the helpless humans.

"Hmm. OK, that's all well and good, but why me? I get that you want to rid the world of vampires and return peace and harmony, and love, etc to the world, but why do I have to do it?" Obsidians voice was ringing with rage now. She just wanted to hear the truth loud and clear she didn't want all the tedious facts that it came laden with.

"You and you alone, are the only one with the power and the strength to do so. The elves' power is weakening, and humans are not physically or mentally strong enough to do it. Don't you realise what you are? As a half elf half vampire, you have the strength and the power of both races" Gaia's voice was full of the power of a hurricane, and she was almost ready to release the power she concealed in it. She stopped herself, however, and regained her composure. After all it wasn't Obsidian's fault she was ignorant to well everything. She had been allowed to run riot almost all of her life with no proper guidance. She had never been taught how to behave.

Obsidian froze. The truth was now seeping in slowly. Rowena placed her hand on her shoulder to offer her comfort, but she pushed her away. She wasn't use to signs of affection.

Torch circled high in the sky above looking for food in distant fields. She flew high enough that the humans could mistake her for an aeroplane. She could not eat the animals in the Forest of Dreams nor did she want to. Those animals were her friends. Obsidian watched as Torch seemed to be flying farther and farther away. She turned to Rowena and with a tear or two collecting in her eyes as she realised Torch was leaving.

Rowena tried to speak. She was also slightly shocked, she didn't know Obsidian was capable of showing actual emotions, let alone that she could truly care enough about something that she could cry.

"Let her go. She can't come to the city with us, but she has a plan of her own, of that I'm sure. She would not just abandon you"

Rowena's words offered little help and even less comfort to Obsidian. As she stood on the barge with her head full to bursting point with all this new information.

She still had questions left to ask though and she knew they could not wait. However she felt a little apprehensive in asking them. In this whole scale of good and evil, of elves and vampires and humans with their so called free will, where did she sit? And if the good went up and the bad went down, if she was half and half, where did she go? If she killed her father, that would be evil, yet she would be doing it for a good reason, to save the humans. So would that be seen as a good act or a bad one? The main thing she really wanted to know was what was her fate, and at the end of the day when all was said and done where would she go? Up? Down? Or sideways?

It was her grandmother who finally spoke, and broke the silence. She was standing on the bank looking straight at Obsidian. None of them were sure how long she had been standing there. She spoke to her as if she had heard all the questions whizzing around inside her head. And her answer, although not very helpful, was all Obsidian had ever really expected.

"No one really knows what will become of you. And until such a time as it has to be decided no one will." With that she turned away from the bank, her head looking up at the sky. She was hiding her longing from the others her longing to be back with her own kind and to put all of her troubles on Earth far behind her. She knew however that they were more present now then they ever had been before that this was really still only the beginning of greater, and worse things yet to come.

Dragon Days

Meanwhile, little known to Obsidian, Torch was heading off to Dragon Isle a small hidden island just off the west coast of the island where this story is based. It lay hidden from human sight by the Almighty One's powers, and almost always was protected by at least one dragon. For it was the chosen place of the mystical and highly sought after Tree of Life, which was believed to be the oldest tree on Earth and maybe all the plants out there. It was in this Tree that Gaia had chosen to hide the secret of eternal life. The secret that was passed to her by the Almighty One, and that he entrusted her to keep forever.

In truth the secret was this, no human could acquire eternal life. It was not possible for humans to live forever. They could only live on as spirits. However, they would only find this out once they attempted to cut down or take a weapon to the Tree. Of course they had to get past the dragons first. If the humans knew the truth to the secret, then the Almighty One feared that the humans would chose to leave Earth, by means foul or fair and live the rest of their days in the Higher or Lower Realms leaving Earth to be desolate and abandoned. For what would the point be in staying if staying only brought death?

Over time, talk of the Tree passed out of stories. It was forgotten or only spoken about by fools who had lost their minds. This was how it should be. This was what would truly keep the Tree safe. For not only did it contain the secret, it contained also all of the life force that kept humans bound to the Earth. If the Tree was destroyed, all of humanity would be destroyed with it. Not even Gaia herself knew this however. For the Almighty one did not fully explain the extent of the secrets power.

It was now Torch's turn to help guard the isle. There were only a few dragons left on the isle. Those that still remained were getting old and had been weakened by the years. As the youngest dragon on Earth Torch had decided it was time she helped out. She finally responded to the call of the dragons that had been haunting her over the years. The older dragons had sensed her when she hatched and realised that they had potential help coming in the form of a younger fitter dragon. There was also the possibility of mating with her and producing a new egg if Torch got there while the other dragons were still able to, well, perform the intricate dragon mating... um shall we say... dance?

The older dragons also felt that she had been shunning her duties by choosing to protect Obsidian. After all she was nothing more than a spoilt elf child to them.

Torch knew the truth though, she sensed it all along. From the first day of her training she knew that greater things than the forest lay in wait for Obsidian. She had just hoped that the day would never come, as she loved Obsidian in a way that the other dragons could never understand, for they had never known love themselves. The whole reason Torch had hatched was to protect Obsidian, however once she found out the plan involved taking Obsidian to the city where the humans lived, Torch felt she could not follow for fear of being hunted down and killed by the barbaric humans. Thankfully her bond with Obsidian was unbreakable, and even as she flew further away from her, she could still feel her presence. Torch could feel everything that Obsidian felt and knew everything she was thinking. Even if Obsidian was never fully aware of Torch's abilities, Torch didn't mind. It allowed her to at least keep her thoughts to herself, and ultimately meant she could keep the dragon's biggest secret of all. The true whereabouts of the Tree of Life. The knowledge about the Tree was instilled in each and every dragon well before they hatched, for it was the real purpose of their existence and the reason Gaia created them, (well, most of them that is), to protect the Tree of life was the reason the dragons lived, and breathed.

The second Torch landed on the isle, she set her fellow dragons straight on a few things.

The first being the reason she hatched. Gaia had created Torch's egg herself and had created her to be the protector of the saviour of the human race. Gaia could always tell that humans where heading for trouble, she just didn't realise that it would be at the hands of a vampire. Gaia was convinced that humans would destroy her beloved Earth, and in turn she would have to retaliate. However she was also convinced that someone would come forward and try to stop the humans. This person would then require protection from the other humans, and what better protection than a dragon? The other dragons rumbled with laughter. How could Gaia be so wrong they laughed?

The next thing Torch set them straight on was Obsidian. Although she seemed spoilt, it wasn't her fault. Her grandmother had given her everything she could wish for, which wasn't much as all she had ever known was her life in the forest. Torch was her only friend, she had Rowena who was more of a tough teacher than a friend, and she didn't respect

Obsidian. She too thought Obsidian was a s[poilt child who] lacked discipline.

Torch explained how Obsidian's grandmot[her had been] afraid to discipline her for fear of retaliation, and was afraid she would spark off her vampire side. So she treated her like a child to try to keep her innocent elf side as the dominant side in her personality. Obsidian hated this, she knew she wasn't a child as she was growing up and would often confine in Torch that she wished she wasn't treated like an idiot all the time. She knew there was something dark in her, but couldn't understand what it was. She wanted to know why her mother was a useless mute, who spent her life in a daze, and never had anything to do with her. She felt lost and unloved.

Once Torch explained this the dragons felt they could relate to Obsidian's plight. The poor thing only wanted answers, only wanted love, and was treated like an over protected child, because she was feared and misunderstood just like the dragons that guarded the isle.

They took some convincing, but once they were satisfied with Torch, and her reasons for staying away from the isle for so long, they allowed her to feast. They still found it difficult to believe that Gaia had created her for a special task; however, they were willing to forgive Torch for what they though was a simple case of bending the truth suit her own needs. She seemed like she could be a little unruly however, she was with them now, and that was all that really mattered.

It worked highly in Torch's favour that dragons could not read each other's thoughts. It would not have been so easy to convince the dragons she was now with them for good if they knew the truth. That she had a connection to Obsidian, even while she was on the isle. She, was ready to leave the second that Obsidian needed her. For although she was on the Isle with her fellow dragons, she felt no connection with them. After all, she did not share the same desire that they did to protect the Tree of Life. In Torch's mind, the Tree could burn for all she cared. All that mattered was Obsidian, and her safety.

The Master Plan?

Far away back in the forest, Obsidian's head was now spinning even more. She now knew what she had to do, and to a point she understood why she had to do it. All she needed to know was how the hell she was meant to do it? She had lots of training, but how much could it really help her against an evil vampire who was created by the devil himself? She wasn't overly keen to find out, but and truthfully in all honesty can you blame her? I know I wouldn't want to do it.

"So does anyone have a plan?" She turned to face Gaia and Rowena, and was not reassured at all when she was met with blank faces. As you can imagine this was not the kind of response she was expecting or hoping for. She felt totally doomed, and not for the first time since hearing her plight and what she was expected to do.

Rowena spoke up. "Well, I have a car, so at least I know how we are going to get to the city. And I have a place to stay in once we get there, and well, that. That's it so far, but it's a start." Rowena once again felt more than slightly stupid, she really should have thought this through more.

True to form Obsidian hadn't lost her sarcasm, even though she had lost all hope. "Oh, great, Rowena, so I'll just drive to the city, then drive around when I get there until I find my dad, and then run him over, shall I? Hmm, brilliant idea, oh, except I can't drive, oh. And don't look so shocked; I learnt about cars in a book in the library. I guess I should have read up on cities, oh, and how to banish evil vampires, and send them back to hell while I was there really, shouldn't I? Silly me." If only there *had* been a book in the library that could help her with this. At least she knew why the books where there now. So she would have some understanding about the outside world. That was how she found out that there was an outside world and it wasn't all make believe.

"Um…" Rowena paused uncertain of how to approach the subject.

"Well yeah um we really need to leave as soon as possible. OK, so we don't have a plan, as such…but um you're

an excellent fighter, and I'm sure when the
you'll know what to do…. And I've um ye
go….I've got clothes and stuff for you at
our place, so all you need to do is make your way to the car…. and leave the driving to me" Rowena tried her best to sound hopeful despite her lack of planning and overall preparations for the task that undoubtedly lay ahead.

Obsidian did not share this flicker of hopefulness and felt as though she could burst in to flames. She could almost feel her blood boiling, and if she got any hotter she was sure that blood vapour would start venting out of her ears.

They didn't have a plan. Great. So they were putting the fate of the human race in her hands in the hope that she would know what to do at the time. Brilliant. She was so angry she didn't even give a thought to the fact that Rowena had scooped her up and made the jump form the barge back to the bank. This was pretty impressive considering the distance. Even the mermaids were left stunned by the act.

Now safely back on the bank of the lake Rowena placed Obsidian down and walked over to a very odd looking car. You or I would know it as an original VW Beetle. Obsidian just gazed at it in wonder for it was nothing like the pictures of the cars she had seen in the books in the library.

at even the stuff she had learned about cars wasn't helpful. She didn't even know if what Rowena was standing by actually was a car.

Rowena read the look on her face, and was suddenly met with an even bigger sinking feeling. Obsidian was totally unprepared for life outside the forest, and although she had dedicated the last few years of her life training her, Rowena had never thought to teach her about the outside world. Hmmm the word *idiot* sprang to mind. Well it was too late now; Obsidian would just have to learn as she went along. For her most part she was a fast learner. When she would shut up and listen that was.

It's a Long Old Road Out of Here

It really was too late to go back now. Rowena and Obsidian were in the Beetle and ready to go. Much to the horror of both of them. They were both filled with a feeling of "shit, we really are fucked" feelings aside, Rowena started the engine, the motion of the car moving did little to settle Obsidian's already unsettled stomach.

There was no road or track to lead the way out of the forest. Rowena had left the forest several times before, but the forest was always quick to cover any tracks left in or out. New plants and flowers would spring up, and the creatures of the forest were always rushing around here and there, especially the fairies and imps, who were always playing tricks on each other. So it was never not long before Rowena's tyre tracks were completely hidden. This had proven to be a total nightmare, as Rowena was never totally sure which way she was going, and could never tell if she was driving around in circles or not. None of the creatures were any help either, you could never trust an imp, no one apart from the fauns spoke faun, and unicorns always talked in riddles. Right now Rowena really didn't have time for riddles, and Obsidian was in no fit state to help out. Her travel sickness was setting in thick and fast.

After a few hours of aimless driving, later Rowena finally caught sight of what she had been looking for. At the edge of the forest was a now derelict, reasonably sized house, situated on the outskirts of the village of New Haven. A long track wound its way up to and beyond the house with fields on either side of it. It was this track that would lead them to the main road, and to the city. It was the same road that Lucy took, and we know where that road led her.

Obsidian was already feeling way beyond nauseous from all the driving around. But by the time they reached the track, it was all too much, and she ordered Rowena to stop the car. When she returned, back to the car she never spoke not a single word, she just sat with her head in her hands. She took deep breaths every time the car went over so much as a stone in the road, but she didn't complain again. She couldn't so much as talk. She daren't, for fear of being ill again. She could certainly do without that right now. In fact, she could do without all of this right now.

It was getting late, so thankfully the roads where quiet. Only a few cars passed them on the way to the city. Every so often a driver would forget to dip their lights, and Rowena would scream abuse at them for temporally blinding her. But other than that, neither she nor Obsidian spoke. Not that either of them had anything helpful to say to the other. But then again, they never had.

Big City Lights.

After a long night of driving, the lights of Georgiana came in to view. Obsidian finally lifted her head, rubbed her eyes, then yawned. Fantastic she was feeling tired now as well as disgustingly sick. She was glad, however, that she had taken the effort to look up, even if she was feeling vile.

"Wow! It looks so beautiful, all the twinkling lights; it looks so magical, and…"

She took another deep breath, and dipped her head back down. It was too much, pretty as the lights were, she was getting a headache due to her tiredness, she guessed.

"Not long now and we will be at my place and you can have some proper rest. No offence, but you look like death." Once again Rowena had tried and failed to say something constructive to the situation.

"hy thank you, you're far too kind." Obsidian ugh but still felt to ill to function. She thought for once she would try and make light of the situation, she was, after all, going to have to get used to Rowena sooner or later if she was stuck with her. This for once was quite a mature thought for Obsidian, maybe she was growing up. Maybe not. Time would tell.

She did occasionally lift her head again to look at all the warm, glowing lights of the city. When she did the thing she couldn't fail to notice was a large patch of red lights to the east side of the city. As they got closer still, she noticed that to the west the lights were light blue in colour. The rest, though, had a warm, friendly glow about them. They were your average, everyday streetlamps, the kind you normally have find right outside your bedroom window, and that glare into your room when you're trying to sleep. You'll find out what the other lights are later, if you haven't worked it out already, that is. The annoying streetlamps were something, along with lots of other things, that Obsidian would have to get use to.

As they reached the city, Obsidian was amazed by the buildings., She had never seen any buildings other than her own home, of course. The buildings in the city were mostly Georgian in style and were made of a light coloured sandstone. They had large windows at the front, and you could see inside. Some had lots of clothes in them, while others housed strange looking household objects. Lamps and computers to the rest of us. Well, I won't bore you with all the details, you can imagine what a normal high street looks like. Along with the main high street, there were back alleys, and streets that led lead off into the darkness. Further on than Obsidian could see there were posh bars, underground nightclubs, a modern cinema complex, and countless restaurants also littered the street, offering food from around the world.

There was so much going on, that Obsidian found it almost impossible to take it all in. There were people everywhere, the streets were crawling in them. Some had pale, hollow complexions like they were lacking in something and had never seen the sun, others were full of life, and alcohol. Obsidian's head was constantly moving from left to right, as her brain tried to take everything in.

Finally, after what seemed like a lifetime of driving, the car began to slow down. It slowed to a stop as it approached a row of buildings shaped in a crescent, with a beautifully exquisite park laid out in front of it. To Obsidian it almost felt like it could be home. Almost. Although she wasn't so sure about the wildlife that chose to inhabit it, especially in the early hours of the morning.

Small groups of teens were sat huddled together smoking things, some legal, some not and all of them were drinking, some soft drinks, some well, you get the picture. I'm sure most of you have been there; don't pretend you haven't. Others were running around singing, dancing, and acting foolish, and some were removing items of clothes, ready for, well, um, other things.

"Hmm, and these are the things I've got to save?" sighed Obsidian, and she dragged her worn- out body toward the buildings, and just that little bit closer to bed. Not that she would be getting much sleep, not this night anyway.

Beautiful Nightmare?

Obsidian paid little attention to the décor of Rowena's flat; she failed to see how spacious and light and airy it was, how big the TV was, or what the artwork was like. She didn't even notice the large damson leather sofa with fluffy cream cushions that Rowena had taken a whole day trying to pick out, and another day trying to get into the flat. All she noticed was the soft fern green painted room with the door slightly ajar and the comfy looking bed inside.

"Hmmm, I take it that room's mine?" she asked pointing sleepily to the green room. Even if it wasn't her room, she didn't care, she was sleeping in that comfy, inviting bed. Or so she thought.

"Oh yeah, it's yours. I hope you like it. Oh, and one more thing before you crash out, I am………. well, I'm going to have to start calling you Sid, or something, as with a name like yours in this city you're going to stand out. Hope you don't mind? And it will be short for Sydney if anyone asks....... right well I er um think that's it... Ooh, one more thing, I'm Charlie from now on, ok? OK? Again I want to be, um, inconspicuous, if you get me." Rowena wasn't even sure if Obsidian was listening to her or not. But now unlike always she didn't care; she was too tired herself to care about anything other than sleep. What did it matter if she had to explain herself all over again tomorrow, It wasn't like that was unusual. Especially with Obsidian's ridiculously short attention span, and bad attitude.

"mmmm Mmm...oh, ok OK, right. got Got you. Charlie it is, I understand, I think, well Well, 'night then, im I'm going to sleep now, hope. Hope you don't mind.? As I look like 'death,' as you so kindly put it, and feel disgustingly ill."

Much to Rowena's surprise Obsidian had been listening, Maybe, just maybe, she was ready to take on the responsibility of the task at hand. Only time would tell.

With that Obsidian went into her new, soft green bedroom, and changed into her night clothes, the baby pink ones that Rowena had kindly left on the bottom of her bed.

Changing clothes only seemed to exhaust her even more, so she gave up trying to stay awake, and crawled under the cosy, warm inviting bed covers. The sudden coolness of the sheets sent a chill down her spine, and made her feel a slight sadness, she hadn't realised just how much she would miss Torch warming up the bed for her. In fact, she hadn't realised how much she missed everything about the forest, and her old life. She took a deep breath, and pushed the thoughts aside. Soon she would be asleep and could dream that just for the night, at least, that everything was back to normal. Her version of normal, anyway.

Unfortunately, for her Obsidian wasn't that lucky. As she slept she had the strangest dream. It was so surreal, and so intense. She could feel everything, and taste the smells in the air. Her senses were aroused and stimulated, so much so that she doubted deep down that it really was a dream. It was as if she had entered the devil's playground, and everything was all set out for her.

When she opened her eyes, she was unsure if she was still asleep or not. What she saw was incredibly puzzling to her. It felt so familiar, but at the same time she knew there was no way she could have been there before. This was not the forest where she had grown up. It was a far cry from that. She blinked and rubbed her eyes, even pinched herself, which hurt a little, but despite all that the setting didn't change. For looking all around, she saw that she was standing in an empty car park; there was an abandoned building, possibly an old factory or warehouse, she couldn't be sure apart from to say it was situated to the far right of the car park. It was seriously dilapidated and looked like it would collapse if you she so much as sneezed on it or even near it. To her left was what we all know as a funfair, but unlike most funfairs it looked sinister and dare say creepy, mostly due to the fact it was totally empty, and devoid of human life. There was no one having any kind of fun in this fair. The lights on the rides and attractions flickered and faded. The music they played, stopped and started and skipped, and repeated this pattern again, and again. Although no where to be seen, you could clearly hear the disembodied sounds of children and adults alike laughing and screaming. Their screams were a tangled mixture of fear and excitement, and their frantic footsteps could be heard running between the rides.

The sweet, enduring smells, of popcorn, candyfloss, and fresh doughnuts tinted the air, there was also an under current of hotdogs, and hamburger vans, and chips that ran along side the sweet smell. Obsidian could literally taste these things in the saturated air, and although she had no idea what the smells and tastes they were, they were as familiar to her as the mermaids in the lake back at home.

Home, a place she wished she was now. If this really was a dream, she wasn't the one controlling it.

Slowly and cautiously she turned towards the fair. It was then that she saw it, a figure moving closer to her, shifting and darting between the rides. It was twisting and flowing through the air like a flock of tiny black birds. Then, in a flash and a flurry, it appeared in front of her. First of all it took the form of a goat, then in it changed to have a goat's head, the feet of a lion, and a griffin at the back with a snake like tail. It quickly altered its shape again to that of a little red demon with a trident and horns. Then another flash and it took the form of something dark and hideous. A creature from the deep surrounded by flames, a creature that had no really distinguishable shape or form, however despite this fact it would haunt and dement your mind nonetheless. Then finally a man, tall, slim build, messy blonde hair light blue eyes. He smiled a captivating smile, and her heart was gone. For he plainly and simply stole it.

They didn't speak, not to start with away. Instead, like sexually charged teens, unsure of how to act, they just exchanged glances, and suggestive smiles. Then he changed tactics, he held out his hand and grabbed hold of her, and then he pulled her near. They kissed, and the whole world went hazy, she couldn't see, but she didn't care. Her whole mind was full of him. Her whole body was taken over. And she was powerless to stop it, not that she wanted to. When

Obsidian finally came to her senses, she was lying naked on the floor in the abandoned car park. The blonde man was standing over her . She felt startled; she was back in her own mind, but still in this dream. She shook her head, tried to wake up. It didn't work.

"Who are you? Where am I? And what's going on?" They all seemed logical questions to ask.

"So many questions? Well, I've shown you what I am, and a glimpse of what I can do, and what you see now is what you want to see. I'm your fears, fantasies, dreams, and nightmares. I don't scare you, though; I can tell that much. From how I look now, I can see you're focusing on dreams and desires. My name well, I have many. Lucifer is my favourite. My business here concerns you, and your little mission. You know what I'm referring too. I could help you, and maybe I will, as it's in my best interests that you succeed. Does it help that I find you alluring? Probably not? Can you trust me? Definitely not. Well, the light is stirring in the sky, and you should be in bed."

Clueless

When Obsidian finally woke up, she was back in her bed, and it was daylight. She wasn't sure what had happened in the night. All she knew for certain was that she was famished; what she didn't know amongst other things, was how to cook. Of all the many things Rowena had taught her, this was the one of the many thing she had missed. One of the things that could really be useful to her right now.

Rowena had already left, however. She had left a note for Obsidian saying she was out making preparation and not to expect her back until late afternoon.

"Hmm," Obsidian said as she rummaged around in the kitchen. "OK, I know what these things are, fridge, oven, freezer. Er Um, weird thing that looks kind of like a TV set, I saw in a book in the library. Don't remember it saying they would be useful in a kitchen, though, or that they open up."

Obsidian opened the cupboards under the microwave, for your information it was not, as she thought, a TV, and rummaged around. They were full of packets of convenience foods, noodles, pasta in sauce, that sort of thing. She opened a packet of the pasta in sauce and started to munch on the contents.

"Ew, what is this? 'Pasta in sauce' Where's the sauce? It's all powdery, and vile. Disgusting. Truly vile. Hmm, beans. I can cook beans. You just pull back this thing here, and to heat them. I wonder. Do they go in here?" She took another look at the microwave and pulled on the handle that opened its door. Finally she was getting the hang of things. Well, kind of.

"Wow!, No no no no no! Don't do that. Metal in a microwave equals bad idea. Very bad idea. Are you trying to get yourself killed? LOL, well, maybe that was a little extreme, but Jesus, for the love of God, woman, what were you thinking?"

Obsidian whirled around in shock. "Lucifer!? What are you doing here? How did you get in? Wait, how did you know where to find me? Am I dreaming? What is going on?"

He leaned forward, slowly placed his hands on her face, and kissed her.

"Did that feel like a dream to you?" he asked the question, although it wasn't a question. Not really, not a proper one.

"Yes, I mean, no, I don't know, I don't understand! Last night? Was it real? Are you real? Is this real?" Obsidian was confused, angry and confused. Not a good combination.

"It's as real as your dreams" He knew the riddle in his words would infuriate her even more.

"OK, stop it! Stop it right now! Stop messing with my head!" It had worked, she was raging now.

"Ooh, but im I'm not in your head, I'm in your kitchen. And I'm not messing with it you are. I mean, look at all the mess you've made, Obsidian." He indicated the microwave. "And with a click of my fingers, see, it's all gone." He snapped his fingers and all the mess Obsidian made had disappeared. "Spick and span. If only all messes were as easy to clean up. This little vampire infestation we have here, now, it's out of control. And the man upstairs, and all of mankind is counting on you to stop it, and you can't even cook beans." He smiled, if he had lit her rage to start with, now he was pouring petrol on the flames now, and loving every second of it. He truly was a pyromaniac. One that was, however, about to get burnt by the very fire he ignited.

Obsidian reached out for the knife block, and before Lucifer could stop her, or even move, she had thrown all the knives at him. But he didn't bleed, he didn't drop a single speck of blood. Obsidian spun around to see all the knives were back in the block.

"Now that was fun We should do that again." Lucifer brushed himself down. There was not a single mark on him.

"How did you do that?" Obsidian demanded. "I mean, I hit you with all those knives, and now they're back in there!" She pointed to him, and then back to the knife block, all the while shaking her head, as if that would help her work out what had just happened. It didn't make sense, but nothing about Lucifer made sense. None of this made any sense.

"Haha, babe, I think you'll find the real question here is, how the hell did you hit me?

I mean, good shot, by the way. But still, I'm mean I'm me, and I'm meant to be untouchable, I am shocked. You got me there, babe, haha, and there." He pointed out all the places where the knives should still be. He was puzzled, too. He was meant to be untouchable. Until now, he was anyway.

Obsidian shrugged. "I'm a good aim, what can I say? But if I can't kill you! You you disgusting, condescending, vile, patronising, what? What are you, by the way? Ew!" Her face changed in horror. "Oh no, we didn't I mean, did we?... And the goat thing, and the horns....ew ew ew ew!" Her sarcasm made way for genuine disgust.

"Flashbacks, my dear? Haha, oh no, don't tell me you regret last night!? Oh, so sorry. Ha. Believe that, and you'll believe I'm the devil." He was full on grinning again. This time he had tiny red horns, and a tail to match.

"OK, drop the act. I need answers. How do I kill him? I mean, what's his name? My father. What is his name?" Obsidian was not impressed, or in the mood for any more tricks or for playing games. This time she meant business, and she wanted answers, so answers she was gonna get no matter what she had to give in return.

"Oh, but we can't give him one," Lucifer replied. "For name equals power. If we give him a name, it makes him more real and gives him more power over us. If you name him, he will find you. And then we will all be doomed. You can't be afraid of something if it's not real, and it can't hurt you if it does not exist. He can't find you if he does not exist. But you can find him." Lucifer wasn't even sure himself if he was talking sense, and when he saw the look on Obsidian's face he knew the answer.

t? I'm sorry, I beg your pardon, but in English he didn't understand him one bit. I can get why.

Lucifer sighed and tried to explain. "One of the few advantages you have over him is that he doesn't know you exist. Another one is that to you he doesn't have a name;, only things that exist have names. But you know he exists, and you don't have to give him a name. If a person names him, he can control them, he can scare them, feed of off them. He becomes their nightmares. But if you don't name him, he is simply another man in the street. He can't touch you or talk to you or harm you in any way. You can refer to him as Father, Daddy, or my darling dad, it doesn't matter, as that's not a name., It's what he is to you. You didn't name him that. It is what he is. He is also a vampire; that's not a name. It's a thing. A father is a thing. But to give that thing a name would make it deadly." He still wasn't sure he was making sense, and he'd made the rules up. If he didn't get it, how the hell could she?

But Obsidian was nodding. "Oh, OK, I think I get it. Right, so if I refer to him as Father, that's fine, because its like saying I'm a person, or this is a chair. It's just an object. If I found a cat in the street, it's just a cat, but if I name it, then it's my pet. It's no longer simply a cat. If I call out its name, it will come to me. It will know who I am. If I don't call its name, it will just pass me by.

"At the moment my father is just some man. I don't know him. But if I knew his name then I would, and he would become that name; and in this case that name is bad, it's wrong, it's evil. If I called out his name, he would come to me. He doesn't know he is my father, so if I say that, he won't come. I get it!

"But if I don't know his name, how can I find him?

"Lucifer? Lucifer?

"Great, just as I was finally getting answers, he leaves. Brilliant!" She still wasn't totally sure she did get it, either.

In the Club

It was dark when Rowena finally made it home.

"We are going out! And when I say *we*, I mean Charlie and Sid, LOL, we sound like two old men. Haha, I love it. I've got you an outfit. It's a killer 'LBD', a li'l black dress, in case you were wondering. Can you walk in heels? Hmmm, well, I got you these. You'll just I have to... um... I don't know, try not to look to retarded in them." Rowena seemed bouncy, and almost positive. Like an overactive puppy that had just gotten a new toy, she was ready to play.

"Um right okay, so what exactly have you been doing all day?" Obsidian was annoyed, after being left on her own for most of the day.

"Yeah, I could ask you the same thing, but I won't, as you've have clearly been inside all day!, Oh, I got you some makeup. Just... um well, I'm sure you'll work out what to do with it. Now go, get ready !" Rowena was getting impatient. What had Obsidian been doing all day, while she had been out making plans? Not that they were much to do with Obsidian, but they would help Rowena.

But Obsidian wasn't finished. "OK, so this L.B.D is going to help me stay inconspicuous, is it? I have a few more questions for you. Now that we're here, I can tell the whole bow and arrow, and sword thing won't fit in. So why did you bother to teach me all that stuff ?" She held the tiny dress in her hand, and used the other one to gesture to the window, and the world outside.

Rowena sighed and leaned against the counter. "Back in the day, its it's how I used to hunt vampires, I would shoot at them with the arrows. If I hit them it would slow them down. Then I would use the sword to stab them through the heart, and cut off their heads. I know in this day and age I need to take a more modern approach, but I still like to practice; it keeps me limber." She wasn't totally telling the truth. It wasn't vampires that she use to hunt. They hadn't been around long enough to see bows, and arrows. Not in this world anyway.

"I think I understand. So nowadays do you do the neck-breaking twists? And karate chops? And run up walls? And do back flips? All that acrobatic fighting, that's what I'll have to use, on the vampires, too, isn't it?" She was thankful she had learned that stuff, too.

Rowena shrugged. "Yeah, pretty much. To be honest most of them have gotten lazy, and complacent in their old age, and they don't bother to learn to do any of that. But they are still pretty fast as fuck. I still can't keep up after all these years. You, on the other hand, won't have that problem. Remember all those times we raced through the forest, and I could never catch you? Not even when you were a child, and all the animals would run away from you? That's the hunter in you. The vampire in you. But being half elf, you made it look so graceful, and so easy. Anyways, that's enough reminiscing. Let's go put our war paint on and, kick some vampire ass! Oh my god, I watch way too many movies!" Rowena still wasn't totally telling the truth, but now wasn't the time for the truth. It was time for action.

Although Sid aged slower than humans, it was still modern times when the vampire problem came to Earth. With that in mind what was it that Rowena used to hunt with her primitive bows and arrows? You'd have to read the story to find out.

Obsidian poured herself into her dress, and managed to apply her makeup with a little bit of help from Rowena.

ok a few laps of the apartment in her high na decided they were ready to hit the town. She also felt slightly smug, for she was sure she could outrun Obsidian in heels. Rowena had lots of practice at running in heels, while Obsidian was still struggling to maintain her usual graceful, effortless stride.

They took the short cut through the park, which was usually teeming with teenagers, doing as I said before, drinking alcohol and smoking. The park was poorly lit, dim, and shadowy but that didn't stop a group of bored young vampires from playing crazy golf. Obsidian was getting herself ready for a fight, but Rowena held her back, saying it was too dangerous as there were so many off them, and that they couldn't risk any of them running off and warning the vampires in town about it.

"You only take them on one at a time, and let me dispose of the pieces, OK, Sid?" she warned Obsidian.

"Sure Charlie! Whatever you say!" Obsidian snapped back angry that she had missed a chance to practice her fighting skills on some real vampires, and something other than Rowena, or an unfortunate faun for a change. If she was really lucky she used to get to practice on a centaur, they where strong and had awful tempers when they were provoked. She smiled when she thought about the forest and Mother Nature's 'experimental creations' as her grandmother called them.

The rest of the walk passed by without much excitement or talking from either of them.

When they finally reached the club Rowena broke the silence.

"When we are inside don't talk to me unless you have to OK? It's nothing personal I just have some extra business to attend to." She was firm and made it clear this wasn't open for debate.

"OK, sure, fine, whatever, just leave me again. I mean, I'll be fine; what's the worst that can happen, hmmm?" But Rowena was already inside, and Obsidian was standing alone outside the club, looking around hopelessly. "Oh great, she's gone in without me," she said to no one. "That's just great!" Obsidian was beyond annoyed with Rowena. However she was curious to go inside and see what a club was really like.

"Don't worry. You'll be just fine. You'll be with me, and something tells me we are gonna have lots of fun."

Obsidian breathed a deep sigh of relief when Lucifer slipped his hand around her waist. She was surprisingly happy to see him.

"Oh..." He pulled her close, almost crushing her, and whispered mockingly in her ear, "...and when we are inside, can you call me Luca? That always confuses people, and I have some, um, important business to attend to. Ha!" rolled his eyes at his last comment.

"Why would you want to confuse people?" Regardless of why, it had worked, as now once more Obsidian was confused.

"You'll see."

With that he ushered her into the club.

The music was loud, that much Obsidian could tell, but what it was she had no idea. All she knew was that people seemed to like to flail their limbs around to it. It reminded her of when some of the creatures in the forest preformed their bizarre mating rituals.

"Why is everyone looking at us?" Obsidian asked. She was feeling very aware of the eyes that were fixed on them. That, and the people in the club were pointing at them, and then whispering to each other. Whispering about them?

"Ha ha-ha! You're an elf woman, don't you have super strength and hearing and stuff? I know vampires do" Lucifer was using that mocking tone he loved to use when he spoke to her. It infuriated her, but on some level she liked it, too.

"Hmmm do you know if I really wanted to I cou your mind?!" she snapped back in annoyance. The music was so loud it seemed to drown everyone out but Lucifer out. it's It was the first time she had admitted she had some powers she was aware off. She had come across the ability by accident once when she was younger. She read a mermaid's mind. Once and never again. She just thought, *Hmm, I wonder what she is thinking*, and before she knew it her mind was flooded with the mermaid's thoughts. She couldn't read everything or everyone's mind, however. As far as we know, she couldn't read Torch's. And she never really bothered to read Rowena's or her mother's was always blocked, which was frustrating. She tried her grandmother's once, and all it said was "tut- tut, keep out."

"Hmmmm hmm, interesting," Lucifer said. "Well in that case, read theirs! It will be much more entertaining, I can assure you that much." He pointed to a couple of people in the corner.

Obsidian closed her eyes, and her face became contorted as she tried to concentrate on scanning the minds in the room.

"Goddammit, you look so attractive when you do that! You should make faces like that all the time., I mean, no one's looking at you now," Lucifer sniggered.

"Oh, stuff you!" Obsidian lashed out and punched him in the arm. She was more than a little out of practice. "I was trying to concentrate."

Lucifer rubbed his arm. "Owwww! That kinda hurt. It pains me to admit it haha, pains me, get it? Anyway, girl, stuff *you*! LOL, you need to learn some proper insults, and when you concentrate you look like you're having a real bad time on the toilet, so you might wanna stop making" he paused and imitated Obsidian's expression "that face."

"Oh, wow, I hear them, I don't really understand, though. Why are they saying and thinking all that stuff? I mean, you're not wearing a tight red dress, you don't have enormous breasts, you're not a skinhead covered in tattoos, or wearing glasses with a stupid floppy fringe. I could go on wooow! You're not naked either." She glanced at him just to double check she wasn't missing something.

"Really? Someone right now is seeing me naked? Ummmm that's hot but a little creepy. Seriously, though, don't you get it? I, like, well, am the devil. These people are all intoxicated, and when they see me they see all their fantasies and desires. Cool, huh?" Well, at least he was impressed by himself.

"So the you I'm seeing now is not real?" Obsidian felt a pang of disappointment. Would she ever see the real Lucifer? Was it even possible to see the real him?

"Babe, I'm as real as you want me to be." Great, he was turning on his, er, charm again.

"Ew! Sleazy. I can't get my head around all this. I need some air"

Obsidian pushed Lucifer away, threw her arms in the air and stormed out of one of the club's side exits. Well, it was a fire exit, really, but no one could hear the alarms going off over the music. If they could, they didn't seem too bothered.

Rowena's on a Mission

Rowena left Obsidian standing outside the club, she was like yeah sure she'll be fine, but regardless of that I have work to do. She had a score to settle, and nothing, not even the fate of mankind, was going to get in her way. All she knew or cared about was that when she was done there would be one less *man* to worry about in mankind.

So here's the score, Rowena had met Zander a few months back. It all started when she was shopping for curtains for Obsidian. Torch had set fire to yet another pair, as per usual, so Rowena took a welcome break from training Obsidian and headed off to the city. That's when she saw him. You see, Zander worked in the curtain store and could not fail to notice Rowena, due to all the recent trips she had made to the store. She had been in rather a lot, but hadn't been buying curtains every time. Mostly this was due to the price, and the fact that a great deal of them were totally hideous. That aside, she was pretty hard to miss, with her slender, long legs, light beech coloured skin and dark oak eyes. All that teamed with her long dreads, made her certainly different.

"More curtains? I'm starting to get worried about you. This is, like, the third time this week you've been in here." Zander tried to sound playful yet casual. He wasn't sure it had worked, Rowena was scanning the store and absentmindedly playing with her dreads.

"Hmm? Oh yeah, the curtains. I'm an interior designer, doing some renovations on a place….. big place, um lots of windows." She wasn't sure she sounded convincing, but the guy, she glanced at his name tag, *mmmm Zander* seemed convinced.

"Oh, I was starting to think you had a thing for me." He tried to keep it cool.

"Oh really." *Shit,* she thought, *now he' is hitting on me!* She glanced up at his face. *Hmm, piercings.* She looked at his arms. *Decent size, nice tattoos. Hmmm kinda cute, all in all, not so bad.* She smiled.

"Maybe I was." She decided that all in all, he didn't seem too bad. She wasn't sure on his choice of career though, but hey, she could work on that. She had set herself much more difficult tasks in the past, and succeeded at them. Surely getting a man to change his dead- end job would be easy. Lost in her own mind for a while, she nodded and smiled at what he was saying, even though she wasn't really listening. He didn't seem to notice.

Lucky for him, his casual yet playful approach to flirting worked, and they swapped numbers. After a few days of exchanging several slightly, umm, *flirty* texts, they hooked up and had a few dates. They had been dating for about a week if that; doing the usual date stuff, going to the cinema, going out for meals, and having drinks. Then once they got all that out of the way, they embarked on what she thought was meaningful if not slightly sexual relationship. He even went as far as saying the L word to her, and they talked of marriage, and kids. Although Rowena knew she could never really marry a human and have a normal life. She was also sure that if he knew the truth, he wouldn't like the idea of shacking up with a tree, but for a while the dream, at least, made her happy. On the flip side, for all she knew anyway he could just be spinning her a line, and telling her what she wanted to hear to get her in to bed. Either way it worked, and she enjoyed playing make-believe.

That was until she found him in bed with a vampire! The one thing she hated more than anything else, and her favourite thing to kill. She stayed calm, didn't say a word, to be honest she was sure they were a little too preoccupied to notice she was even there. In true Rowena style, she would take her time, and plot her revenge. She didn't want to rush that, like she had with the whole relationship. She was going to make him regret the day the tried his luck with her. And boy, would he regret it!?

She did some research, which thankfully didn't take long, she was a busy girl, after all, and found out the vampire in question was also a barmaid at Obsession. This also only happened to be the hottest new nightclub in town. Not only this, it was the new favourite place for vampires to hang out and lure in unsuspecting, and slightly worse for the wear humans. So she thought it was about time she paid this new hot spot and vamp hive a little visit. After all, she was long overdue a good night out and couldn't recall the last time she'd let her hair down. She wasn't going to let the fact she was meant to be babysitting Obsidian crash her ideas, or her plan. *Not tonight, anyway*, she thought to herself.

Once inside it didn't take her long to spot her. Or him. He looked different, his eyes were distant, and his pupils were enlarged. His skin seemed pale. He was almost twitchy and seemed uneasy around people.

"Damn, that bitch changed him, Oh well, it will just make my job easier." Rowena smiled with a look of satisfaction on her face.

It took a lot for a vampire to change a human. Not only did they have to drink each other's blood, but it was lesser known fact that the vampire also had to suck out the human's soul, and send it on a one way ticket to hell. It was sort of like a down payment on becoming a vampire. You can see why they would want to keep that part a secret. No one would truly want to part with their soul if they fully understood the implications of it. The newly turned vampire would then feel almost lost and empty, it would feed on blood and souls in order to survive. Although vampires could satisfy the lust for blood and feel full for a while, by draining humans. However the blood would die inside them and dissolve, as they had no way of sustaining the nutrients, or oxygen in it to keep it alive, if you will. For their bodies were dead, and their organs ceased to exist in a dead shell. Nothing could live inside them. Also, they could never keep the souls of the humans they drank from; once the body died, the soul passed on, so the desire for a soul was never satisfied. It was little wonder that the human population seemed doomed, what with these helpless, starving creatures seeking them out, and sucking them dry.

"Poor, bastard. Time to put him out of his misery" Rowena said, with a smile on her face that couldn't hide her emotions. It was a look of pure excitement.

She flicked back her hair, and winked in his direction. It worked he was walking over to her. He was gaining some of his memories back; although the body was dead its memories remained, ingrained in their every cell. Vampires had to fight hard with themselves in order to gain access to their memories, they had to really want to remember who they were. Only then would their memories be released. Not only that, but it took a while for newly turned vampires to remember how to act human again and realise they'd had lives before. So few had the chance, what with Rowena around, to hunt them down.

"Charlie, right? The curtain girl?"

Curtain girl! Rowena was seething. *That's how he remembers me?, Well, I'll have to jog his memory a bit.*

She leaned over and in full view of the vampire behind the bar, kissed Zander, running her hands all over his body.

"Wanna take it outside?" she whispered breathlessly in his ear, while she seductively stroked the inside of his leg.

She led him outside, her hands all over him, and he was all over her. His vampire girlfriend did not look happy, and Rowena was sure she would follow them outside. They slipped out through a fire exit that had been opened to let out some of the heat in the club.

In the alleyway she pushed Zander against the wall, kissing him passionately. She could feel his hands moving up the inside of her thigh, and breathed deeply when they reached the silky fabric of her underwear. Just as his fingers pushed the fabric aside, Rowena placed her hands around each side of his neck, and with a quick twist he was demobilised. It would take him awhile to figure out how to fix himself again, and by that time it would be too late. She held him close, feeling the full weight of him on her, and she could feel tears collecting in the corners of her eyes. Before she could let her emotions get the better of her, she saw something move, and, with a sideways glace saw the barmaid, who had also slipped out of the fire exit, shutting it firmly behind her.

When she saw Rowena holding Zander's limp body, she hissed, showing her fangs, and lashed out with her sharp nails, but Rowena was ready for the attack and quickly moved aside. She threw Zander to the floor and grabbed the vampire by the arm, twisting it behind her till it snapped. She forced the struggling barmaid on to her knees; then using her free hand she grasped her face just under her chin and twisted her head until her neck also snapped. Rowena tossed the barmaid aside next to Zander. She felt slightly annoyed that neither had proved to be a good fight, but for her the best bit was still to come.

It was then she began the transition from her human form to her tree form. She needed to be quick, for although she broke the vampire's necks it wouldn't take them long to heal and wake up again. You had to put a stake through their hearts, and cut off their heads to really kill them. But Rowena had her own way of dealing with these two.

When she was fully transformed into a tree, she caught hold of the awakening vampires with her roots. They struggled to break free, but the wood burned into their skin. Wood is deadly to vampires, but only to those created on Earth. The more they struggled, the tighter Rowena squeezed. Her roots were ironically sucking the newly stolen life out of the vampires, and feeding her. When she grew tried of them resisting, she slightly loosened her grip on them and cast them aside. She felt like playing with them, and watched as they untangled their crushed bodies like marionettes coming to life, or a squashed spider regrouping its parts and unfolding itself. The movements were slow and puppet like, and like a puppet master Rowena watched them doing their hideous dance. She was waiting, her roots poised, ready to strike, then just as they had almost healed, she staked them through the heart using her own roots. Blood soaked her roots as she drained the two vampire carcasses dry. Her remaining roots were whipping the skin and flesh from their bones and sucking it up from the walls and ground where it landed. The bodies where almost reduced to bone by the time Obsidian and Lucifer showed up.

Rowena didn't notice them, or the horrified look on Obsidian's face as she crushed the bones to dust, and sucked up the particles with her roots. There was not a trace left of either of the vampires, apart from their clothes, of course. When Rowena was done, she transformed back into her human form. She was, of course, totally naked. Her clothes were miraculously neatly piled up in a corner of the alleyway. She didn't want them to get ruined in the process.

"Allow me" swooned Lucifer as he brushed past Rowena's naked body, on his way over to her clothes.

Rowena turned crimson and let out a sigh as she felt the gentle touch of his clothes on her skin.

Slightly confused by her choice of underwear Lucifer picked up her thong and strapless bra.

"Now surely these don't cover all of that?" he teased as he gestured at Rowena's ample breasts and pert behind.

"Well, ain't you the charmer?" she sassed back with a smile and a flick of her dreads.

All the flirting was getting a little too much for Obsidian to take, so she spun around round and made her way back into the club. However, the mixture of pumping beats and grinding bodies, made her feel much worse. She needed to get out so made her way through the bodies to what she thought was the main exit, and the same way she came in. Instead she found herself in another alleyway. It was dimly lit by a flickering streetlamp. In an odd way it reminded her of a firefly having a seizure. She smiled at the strangely funny image she had in her head, and set off in the direction of what she thought was the main street.

Park Nightlife

After hours of what felt like aimlessly walking up and down streets littered with the dregs of the night's partygoers, Obsidian admitted defeat. She was well and truly lost, so all that was left to do was swallow what was left of her already dented pride and ask for directions. She was so angry with herself; as she never got lost in the forest, ever.

"Um, excuse me, which way is it to the park? You know, the one with the crescent shaped building?"

"Errrr Up there, then make a right, then................."

She didn't catch the rest but headed off up the street and took a right, then a left.

Before long she was lost yet again. Nonetheless, after asking a few more of the night's assorted characters, and deciphering their directions, she found the park.

It was deserted. All the teen vampires that normally populated it were gone. The whole place was overshadowed by an ominous, giant oak tree. Which, if it wasn't for Obsidian's amazing eyesight would have blacked out all that was left of the moon and the streetlights' pathetic attempts at illuminating the area.

She had never noticed the oak tree before, which stood all on its own in the middle of the vast expanse of grass in front of the crescent- shaped building. Hmm, she pondered, had it been there all along and she had never even seen it? Her eyes made one more lap of the park. OK, she guessed it was possible that she had never really noticed much about it before, there were some ruins of a bandstand, plenty of trees and lots of animals, and... *What's this?* Her eyes found something new and much more exciting to look at than some tree. She stopped and found herself staring.

He was young, well into his teens. A vampire. Hmm he looked about seventeen, she guessed. As she stared at him, images of Rowena and Lucifer entwined in each other filled her mind. She needed something to get that image out of her head, and that something was him. His hair was messy and fell in an asymmetric fringe other his left eye, as he flicked it back she noticed he had dark hazel eyes, that gradually turned to red at the edges, like a dry, burning leaf. His lips looked so inviting, and she was sure that for a second she could see through and catch a glimpse of what was beneath his clothes. All she could see was perfection. Her mind was filled with him. Before she knew it she was standing in front on him.

She wanted a kiss, just one kiss. She didn't even know why she wanted it so bad. Was it the hurt or betrayal she was feeling, or did she just want revenge?. She didn't know; all she knew was she was sitting on top of him kissing him. The kiss seemed strangely familiar, not like kissing some random vampire she had never met before. Everything about it screamed, *You know this kiss, you know theses hands that are making their way up your thigh.* She gave up thinking; she didn't care she let him take control. Control of her, of the situation, and of her body. It wasn't untill she found her self undoing his belt buckle and reaching inside his jeans that she stopped herself. Then he pulled her closer, kissing her more intensely than ever, and touching her so she wanted him more. She pulled away, this time not because she wanted to stop but because she had to breathe. He kissed her neck with, one hand between her legs the other undoing her bra. She decided to try again and slipped one hand inside his jeans. It was then he said it. It spoiled the moment and totally burst the bubble of ecstasy she was in.

He said, "I want to ride you like a cheap fairground ride, hard and fast with lots of screaming. All you gotta do is scream if you wanna go faster!"

Obsidian pulled away from him and opened her eyes. She was sitting on Lucifer

"Oh, come on, babe, I was enjoying your kinky little fantasy. Remember, I only give you what you want, and right now I'm guessing that ain't me." Despite his playful tone, he was surprisingly hurt. He would never let on, though. I mean, was the devil able to get hurt? Surely not. But this wasn't the first time she had wounded him. Only this time it was different. It wasn't with a knife; it was emotions, feelings, and false accusation

"You....you!" She gasped furiously.!!! "Had sex with my best friend! Well my only friend! How could you? Well, I know how you're a heartless bastard demon fuck from hell, that's how!" She was hitting him tears streaming down her face.

It was then that Lucifer noticed the colour of her eyes for the first time. They were violet, bright violet. He saw the colour of her hair in the moonlight; it wasn't black, not true black, but had a red hue to it, like the colour of CocaCola. She was still screaming, and he was looking at her skin, her soft, sand coloured skin, her rose pink lips, a strange beauty like this wasn't made for this world. He thought of sirens and how they brought down ships. She was a tragic beauty, one that could destroy men, and worlds. No wonder she didn't fit in here. *Yes,* he thought now laughing, *she is still screaming, and hitting me.*

"Don't laugh at me! Don't fucking laugh at me!"
If only she understood why he was laughing.

But he said only, "Swearing now, oh. I see how my good influence is wearing off on you."

"Fuck you, and go back to hell!"

With that she turned and ran back to the apartment.

No Time for Lies

Rowena was sitting on the sofa in her pjs when Obsidian burst in.

"Well?" Rowena asked quizzically.

"Well, what?" Obsidian shot back.

"Did you see, it?" Rowena asked hopefully.

"See what? Oh you mean you sleeping with my ....um, well, with Lucifer. Yes I saw." Still caught up in her own anger, Obsidian misunderstood Rowena.

"What the...? You know what? Nevermind. I was going to tell you all about how we kicked the asses of those vampy teens in the park, about how I turned into a massive oak tree and finished them off, and about how Lucifer sent them screaming and begging back to hell. But you obviously don't wanna hear it, so fuck you, and your ridiculous accusations." She was angry now, and hurt.

"Um, yeah, whatever, I don't need to hear this right now. I'm off to bed! Don't wake me in the morning as I won't want to see you. OK!? Oh and I got lost and spent the best part of the night wandering the streets asking vagrants, and street minions for directions, but I'm OK, really, thanks for asking!"

With that both girls stomped off to their rooms, slamming their doors closed behind them for effect.

The Mourning After

Rowena woke up, still angry about how Obsidian could accuse her of such a thing. Not that Lucifer and Obsidian were exclusively dating or anything. But still, she didn't want to think about it. She needed to clear her head. She needed to get out of the flat. She showered, dressed, and left. All before Obsidian had even stirred, or showed any attempt at waking up.

When Obsidian did wake up, she found Lucifer sitting on her bed.

"Oh, you! And what do I owe the displeasure? I mean, if you have come to apologise, don't bother, Rowena has already assured me nothing happened. I mean, I'm not entirely sure I believe her, she said you were vampire hunting or something? Anyway, what do you want? You know? It doesn't matter. I need a shower." She wasn't really sure what she needed, she just wanted him gone.

Lucifer raised an eyebrow. "Oh, you need a shower? Hmm, so what did you get up to last night? While you were getting all hot and heavy with the vamp teen, so don't talk to me about being honest or whatever. But as you seem to want to believe that, well, all I can say is be careful what you wish for. I just might get it for you. See ya!"

She got her wish, he was gone.

* * *

Her head still buzzing, Rowena mindlessly wondered the streets of the city, not really sure how she was feeling. Was she angry? Hurt? Or just too full of angst ridden teenage vampire blood that she couldn't really feel anything?. She needed something to clear her head, and settle her stomach. She was hungover on over indulgence.

She pushed her way through the crowd, and headed down a quieter, darker, side street. She wandered past handbag shops, cookie shops, shoe shops, a silver shop. An apothecary? It seemed to appear from nowhere, and answered all her prayers. She had never seen it before, but then again, she had never been looking. She pushed the door open, and casually stepped inside. The apothecary was deserted, dusty, and had an intriguing aroma. It was a bouquet of cherry blossoms, and honeydew, and coal dust, and sweet almonds. The scent drifted around her head intoxicating her. A man appeared behind the dusty counter.

"Ahh, overindulged a little, have we?" he asked, the question although he already knew the answer.

As for his appearance was tall and slender, with short-cropped, dark brown hair, and hazel eyes. There was something about his eyes, they had a fury behind them that burned with passion and rage.

"I have just the then thing for you," he carried on talking as if he were oblivious to the way Rowena was gazing at him. With a flick of his wrist he presented her with a small vial of pink liquid.

"Drink it all up like a good girl now, and you'll be as right as rain in no time." He spoke knowingly.

Without thinking twice, or even asking what it was, Rowena pulled off the top and put the bottle to her dark cherry red lips. He was right; she did feel better instantly. She also felt something else. A burning desire to kiss him, this man, a total stranger she had never met before. Yet here she was, in his apothecary, kissing him over the counter. Her head was a rush with feelings, deep, intense feelings for him, and longing for him. She opened her eyes, and the room was spinning and whirling around her. Feeling dizzy, she closed them again, but no matter how hard she tried, she couldn't break away from his lips. Finally she opened them again, and pulled away from him. Feeling slightly confused, she was naked on her bed in the apartment, with the man on top of her.

"ahhhhhhhhhhhhhhhhhhhhhhhhhhhhhhhhhhhhhhhhhhhh!" She let out a high-pitched scream, that sent Obsidian running in to the room. What she saw was Lucifer entwined in Rowena.

Rowena blinked and screamed again;, what she saw was the devil between her legs.
Shocked and lost for words, Obsidian stumbled backwards out of the room. When she slammed the door shut and slinked down against her own bedroom door, she heard Rowena shouting

"Lucifer, you fuck! How could you? Get the hell out and stay the fuck away from me, you creepy fuck!!!!"
she screamed fueled by anger at the top of her lungs.

Obsidian peeled herself up off the floor and decided to seek solitude in her bedroom. She did not expect, nor did she want to see, a very sorry looking baby goat sitting on her bed. It looked like a cute, soft toy. Its big red eyes blinking up at her, long lashes flickering. She scoped the goat up, surprised by how light it was. Made her way over to the window, she opened it and throw the goat out. On its quick decent to the ground, it bleated, "Beeee carefuuuullll whattttt yyyyouuuuuu wwwwisssssh fffffffoooooorrrr!"

It vanished in a black flash before it hit the ground.

Numb

Obsidian slumped down on her bed. All she could hear was Rowena's annoying incessant sobbing and mumblings. Curious as to what the hell she was going on about, Obsidian jumped up off her bed and walked over to Rowena's room. She pushed the door open just enough so she could hear what Rowena was saying. What she heard was very unsettling.

"Oooh, what's happened to me? I've messed everything up. I'm a friggin' tree goddess, the only tree goddess, and I'm meant to look after the trees. Fine, I can do that. But I'm also meant to be this amazing frickin' warrior and train this useless lazy fuck to kill some super strength vampire fuckin' king or lord of something. When Gaia made me and made me a goddess cuz she couldn't cope with looking after everything on this shitty flippin' hellhole, she promised me a mate. But nooo, the sun and moon had to go and mess it up for the rest of us, I mean, it was a total eclipse most of the time with the things they would get up to. It was twenty-four/seven darkness. So of course the Almighty One had to intervene and separate them, and now they only come together once in a blue moon. Ha ha, get it?"

Obsidian was now feeling increasingly worried about her friend, and the fact she was having a total meltdown, and seemed to be talking to herself. She pushed the door open and saw Rowena holding a small teddy bear with bright red eyes. Lucifer. Full of rage, she went to step forward, but the bear shushed her and mouthed, "She's getting to the good bit. Oh, I do love Rowena's little breakdowns"

Obsidian shook her head in disbelief and slipped out of the room. When she turned around, Lucifer was standing behind her smiling, "Oh relax. She has one of these every few decades or so, the last one was hilarious, oh I'm all alone killing things for the fun of it, I'm evil, blah, blah, blah,. I'm stuck here because fuckin' Gaia made me, not the Almighty One, blah, blah, fucking blah, I'm made of wood to stake vampires, fuck, fuck, fuck. LOL, you get the picture, right?" He wasn't sure if she did or not.

"Um, what? I'm confused, Gaia made her?" Obsidian pointed to Rowena's room

"Yeah, and the mermaids and nymphs, and other weird shit you have in that forest of yours. The Almighty One made a whole load of gods to do stuff for him, that he was too lazy to do himself. Like me. Gaia's a laaazzzzy bitch, so she asked for help, and he was like, yeah, sure, why not. So he let her make a bunch of things, Miss Meltdown in there being one of them. His only clause being that they are bound to the Earth and can't go up there, as they were made her, by the Earth, if ya get me?" He oozed his oh so irritating sarcastic tone

"OK, yeah, I think I got ya!" Obsidian replied, mocking Lucifer's sarcastic tone.

"Anyways, I have just about had enough of this up here, down there, Earth sucks shit! And I need some air., I'd appreciate it if you stayed away from me, and left me, to do my thing, as they say."

He was gone again.

A License to Steal

Dressed in casual jeans, pumps, and a vest top, Obsidian decided to hit the streets. She didn't care if she lost herself in the labyrinth of consumerism that surrounded her. She wanted to get lost. She didn't care if she never got found. She craved something, a sense of normality, she was fed up with all the crazy talk, and theories that had poured down her throat lately. She was in the city now, and intended to make the most of it.

When she reached the shops, she laughed more to herself than out loud. She didn't have any way of purchasing any of the pretty new stuff she saw laid out in the windows in front of her. She had read about money, and credit cards, and she knew that was what she needed to obtain all these things. Shoes, dresses, handbags, soap! She paused, shaking her head in disbelief; there was a whole shop dedicated to soap.

Then she thought of something. When she was back in the club, she could read people's minds. But could she do anything else? What was the true limit of her power? Amused by the soap shop, she decided to go inside. The strong scent of so many different kinds of soaps almost made her sick. Obsidian's head was swimming with smells, not at all pleasant to her very sensitive nose. Concentrating hard, she learned not to focus on the smells but on something else.

One of the shop assistants approached Obsidian.

"Lovely day again, isn't it?" *Hmm, what a freak., I mean, check out those contacts. Who wears shit like that out in the daytime? Cyber-goth? Maybe.*

"Um, yeah, it's a… yeah, a great day, I guess." Obsidian responded, feeling a little taken aback by the girl's thoughts. It was the first time she had heard what someone thought of her appearance. She wasn't hurt or upset, more angry that this girl had judged her based on the colour of her eyes. This was going to make stealing soap from her so much easier.

Obsidian turned around and grabbed a handful of the sweetest, most expensive soap she could find. The assistant tried to offer advice, but Obsidian just ignored her.

She didn't care what was good for sensitive skin, or freaks with her bizarre complexion. When she had amassed a sizable amount of soap in the basket the shop assistant had retrieved for her, Obsidian decided to start on phase two of her plan. If she could read people's minds, could she also plant information in them? She was about to find out.

She projected from her mind to that of the assistant, that she had already paid for the soap. She also planted an image of a blonde girl with vivid blue eyes into the assistant's mind. If she was going to think of anything about the person who stole all her soap, it would be about her eyes. Her freaky *BLUE* eyes.

After planting the thoughts and images, Obsidian also found she could remove memories, and thoughts from the girl's head. Wiping her mind completely of any trace of herself, a very satisfied Obsidian left the shop.

Now worried that people would have seen her, she scanned the minds of the people in the street. Anytime anyone so much as looked at her, she grabbed the image straight from the person's mind and destroyed it. After a few minutes Obsidian realised she could do this with very little thought or effort. So she decided it was time to carry onshopping. Due to the fact that she had acquired so much soap, Obsidian decided it would be fun to pay for things with soap. She convinced the shop assistants that soap was really the new currency. Using soap she obtained several pairs of shoes, a few new tops, and some skirts, all using soap, and the power of her mind. Mostly it was down to the power of her mind.

When she was shopped out, and out of soap, she decided to take a breather. It was then that she felt a tap on her shoulder. Without even turning around, she knew it was Lucifer.

"Hmmm Having fun, are we, well? Well, nice to see your putting your many fascinating talents to good use. Just to warn you, though, stealing is a crime, as well as a sin."

Obsidian rolled her eyes. "Oh, who cares?, I guess I'll be going to hell anyway, so I might as well have a little fun on the way there."

"That's my girl." Lucifer smiled, whilst thinking he could use someone in hell with Obsidian's many talents. His current girlfriend in the Under World was fun enough, but her powers were limited, if present at all. He needed someone with more strength, and more attitude. Plus, he hated to admit to himself, but he really was starting to actually like Obsidian. Although initially he had just been using her, now he was starting to feel something for her. If he was really honest with himself, he would have admitted to having feelings for her sooner.

Shit. She was staring at him, and she didn't look pissed off. Did that mean she couldn't read his mind?

"Hello, Earth to Lucifer!" she was calling to him. He breathed a sigh of relief, (she couldn't) before deciding to make a quick exit.

Obsidian was left alone, wondering if she had really been talking to herself all this time. Then she looked up and noticed something on the corner of one of the buildings. It was a CCTV camera. She had read something about them in a book about the modern day use of the camera.

"Fuck." She was now very aware that all of her antics had been caught on camera. Little did she know that when she was sending and receiving thoughts, some kind of power, or frequency was generated that had wiped the cameras recordings. Lucky for her. Shame she didn't know it.

Now convinced she was in big trouble, she headed down one of the side streets and decided to keep a low profile. She also decided to ditch the clothes she had stolen, as she was suddenly having an attack of guilty conscience. Part of her elf sense of compassion was kicking in, and she was feeling bad for the fact that by stealing from these people, she had put their jobs at risk. Also, by stealing thoughts from them, she had formed some kind of bond with their emotions. Unsure of what was really happening or what to do with the link, she opted to switch off all her emotions and carry on walking. This for now seemed like the easier option for now. Lucky for her, the vampire in her allowed for her to do this, not that she ever really tried it out until now. The vampire side of her nature was something she had never really toyed with before.

Vamp it Up

How much could she really do? How much were they keeping from her? "The" being her grandmother, and Rowena. She now knew she could really read, and control minds, although not without consequences. However, she could also switch off also the annoying pity vibes she was getting from the humans. In fact, she could switch off all her emotions, which was amazing. She had let her soft, caring elf side rule her while she was in the forest surrounded by cute and, fluffy, if not slightly strange, animals. Up until a day or so ago, she too, had been one of those animals. Or so she thought. Now she was a step above them, she felt better than them. Her cocky vampire attitude was now in full swing. Well, she'd always had a bit of an attitude, and hated being told what to do. Now she knew why, her dad was in command of an army of vampires, he had successfully tricked his way out of, hell and was now running the show on Earth. No wonder she didn't fell like she had to answer to anyone. Why should she?

She was fast, too, faster than any other creature she had come up against. Even Rowena, who was a nymph or whatever. She could outrun humans, that would be like a skip in the park to her racing one of them. She laughed; it wouldn't even be a race. It would be humiliating, to the human, that is. Not her. She was above that. Nothing could humiliate her. Not now. Not in this frame of mind.

So what if she looked strange to them. Humans were nothing great to look at anyway. Plus they were stupid, and slow in more than one way. That's how vampires were able to trap them, and trick them into turning. If you think about it, you probably don't even need mind control to trick a human. They are so dumb they would probably believe anything you tell them anyway.

Obsidian was well and truly wrapped up in her inner vampire, tapping into all those thoughts that she had suppressed for so long. She felt a rush of relief. It was like she had finally found herself. Like she truly made sense now. She had never really related to her elf side, after all, it held her back. What had it ever done for her mute of a mother? Or her weakening grandmother? It was the vampire in her that kept her strong, not her weak, feeble elf side.

Lost in her thoughts, and in her own mind, she was totally unaware of the fact she was also lost, literally. She was so consumed with her own inner conflict, that she took no notice of where she was going. She didn't even seem to mind. After all, she had bigger issues on her mind. Like why she hadn't explored her vampire side before. Maybe because no one had thought to tell her about it, was the obvious answer that she came to. This further fueled the anger and hatred inside her, bringing out her darker side even more. Unbeknown to her, it was the fear that her grandmother, and Rowena had had of this side that stopped them from bringing it up. They didn't want her to explore it, or use it until they were sure she was ready to use it in a controlled way.

Lucy, Lucy, Lucy

"Oh, Lucy."

"That's not my name, but I'll be Lucy for you," a girl droned in a soft west county accent.

Obsidian froze, unbeknown to her she had walked into vampire land. This was a whole new kind of red light district. Pinned by a sudden, unexplainable fear, she clung to the red brick wall behind her. Around the corner was something she didn't want to see. But just like a curious cat she couldn't help but sneak a peek.

A girl of about sixteen who was dressed in next to nothing, pulled up her barely there micro miniskirt. She flipped her long, dry, bleached hair to one side and exposed her neck, which was covered in bite marks. She was far from a natural blond; Obsidian noted that her roots were almost down to the tops of her ears, and her eyes were dark brown. Her pale skin was marked all over.

Obsidian then turned her attention to the man in the alley with the blond girl. With one glance she knew who it was. She was so close to him, that she froze. She was totally unprepared. Now that she was here in the moment, could she honestly do it? Could she really kill her own father? Even with her newly exposed vampire side, she didn't think she could. After all, despite everything, he was father. With this thought in her head, her vampire strength, and self-assuredness seemed to have abandoned her. She was the weak, pathetic, useless elf again.

All he kept saying was "Lucy, my sweet, sweet Lucy." Obsidian looked away as he dug his teeth into the blond girl's neck. She seriously didn't need to see this. The girl moaned more in pleasure than pain as she writhed around on him. Obsidian could feel a sick feeling rising up from her stomach, she wanted to run, to get as far away from the situation as she could. But she was stuck, held as if by invisible cement to the spot. Pulling on all of her strength, and willpower she freed herself from the force that compelled her to stay. She just wanted to talk to him, she had so many questions, so much she wanted to ask him. She knew she it wasn't possible, not now, not ever. She told herself, *You can't reason with the unreasonable.*

"Oh, Lucy" was all she could hear as she slowly walked away. Lucy, Lucy. Her mother's name had never seemed so annoying, or distracting to her before. She needed a clear head from all the confusion. Why was he saying her mother's name? Why did he still care about her, and still after all this time? She was thinking too much, and was still too close to him, she wasn't ready not right now to deal with any of this, and she didn't want to risk getting seen or caught.

Then, suddenly, it all went quiet. The moaning had stopped. Something new besides thoughts filled her head, a scent. Warm. Intoxicating. It was calling to her. Without thinking she turned back and walked in the direction of the alluring aroma.

"Please god, no! No more, I can't. I don't have much to give, and I... I..." Her soft voice was weak. But the smell. That smell. Was blood? Obsidian looked down to see the girl glaring up at her. Her eyes were wide and begging. She was begging. It wasn't until Obsidian ran her tongue over her full, pale pink lips that she felt them. The thing the girl was so afraid of. The thing that broke her skin, and stole the life from her. Her teeth. Two long, sharp teeth.

"Oh oh my god, I'm *soo* sorry!, Really, I..., I didn't mean to! I" Not really sure what she meant, Obsidian turned and ran, faster than she had ran in a long time. She kept one hand over her mouth. Not that anyone would have seen her, she was a blur.

Hardly out of breath, she burst through the door of the flat, unsure why it had been left slightly open.

"I saw him!" she blurted out.

Rowena rose from the sofa and stared straight at her.

"OK, I know I acted crazy earlier, just a minor freak-out, but seriously! What the fuck is up with your teeth?" She was shocked more than scared.

"Er, shit, yeah, these things. Oh crap, how do I get them to go away?" Obsidian was panicking, this had never happened to her before.

Perhaps unsurprisingly, Lucifer was there in the room with them. "It's just like morning glory; it can go away on its own, but will go away a hell of a lot quicker if you use it. And, Rowena, what is that smell? Ew, eating god- awful processed human shit; don't you crave something human? Well, ladies, I know just the thing. Dial- a- whore, or *donor* as they like to be called. Missy Scaredy-Cat here saw a low- rent one earlier, but I'm sure I can do better than that." With that Lucifer was gone, again.

Obsidian shook her head in disbelief. "What the? Anyway, Rowena, as I was saying or trying to, if these teeth would just fuck off!" She was finding it hard to talk with her new fangs fully extended.

"Ladies, ladies, please!" Lucifer was back this time with a tall, thin girl with long hair dyed bright red. She was wearing lacy red underwear that matched her hair perfectly.

"Now, isn't this more like it?" Lucifer pushed the girl forward.

"No, I'm getting nothing," Obsidian responded, feeling slightly puzzled.

"Oh, I'm sorry." The girl lifted her wrist to her mouth, then bit down hard.

"That better?" She swooned as she offered her wrist to Obsidian.

Without a second thought, Obsidian rushed forward and clamped her jaw down hard on the wrist. She felt something magical flowing down her throat. The warm, sweet taste of life. The girl left out a deep moan, and Obsidian looked down to see that Lucifer had joined in on the fun.

Feeling a tad overdressed she to decided to strip down to her underwear. She felt a new lease on life rushing through her. She could feel everything, including what the girl was feeling, and it felt good. Not wanting to ruin the scene with her mismatched underwear, Obsidian took those off, too. She felt an urge to want to kiss this girl, so she slipped a leg over Lucifer, who was still down on his knees, pulled the girl close, and kissed her.

It was then that Rowena came back in to the room, dressed in next to nothing.

"Well, there ain't much meat on her, but what there is, is mine!"

As she stood behind the girl, Rowena's hair began to wrap around her like tendrils of ivy. With Obsidian's teeth making holes all over her body, and Rowena's dreads wrapped around her, the girl didn't stand a chance. Lucifer was doing all he could be please her, but Obsidian could feel her pleasure turning to agonising pain. She stumbled back, taking Lucifer with her. Looking up horrified, she saw Rowena in a half- human, half- tree like state leeching the life out of the girl.

"Awww, fuck." Obsidian clenched her teeth. "It's no good. I can feel her pain, and I can't let Rowena kill her!"

"Oh, oh ooops." Lucifer giggled. "Yeah, that's your compassionate elf side in you, if you kill anyone you'll feel their pain. Elves are tuned into human suffering;, it's another reason they feel so compelled to help the helpless. I guess you only feel their pain and suffering inside, when you have them inside. Shame; you look hot when you're feeding!"

"AHHH! SHUT THE FUCK UP! Would you? And stop her!"

Trying not to laugh, Lucifer rushed over to Rowena, not entirely sure how to stop a tree goddess mid feeding frenzy. He stood in awe of her power. Obsidian was writhing in pain, and anger, she had never felt so helpless.

"Lucifer, you prick! Fucking do something!" Obsidian yelled out as the pain flooded through her.

Her final scream seemed to shake him out of his trance, and he grabbed hold of Rowena. Unsure what to do next, he bit her on what he believed to be one of her arms, although it looked more like the branch of a tree. Rowena let out a shriek of pain and threw her treelike limbs around Lucifer. But when she ripped through his flesh, it burned her, and she cried out in pain.

Finally able to move again, Obsidian ran over to the girl, who was reduced to a bleeding mass on the floor. She shook her and tried hard to find a sign of life in her. Finally the girl lifted her head, and tried to open her eyes. When she did she saw a vampire, the devil, and a tree demon, or at least that's what she thought she saw, and OMG, could she scream!?

"What the fuck is with woman and screaming? God, do you just spend your whole lives faking it or something?" Lucifer was starting to lose his patience with the whole situation.

Obsidian was running low on patience, too, and her anger levels were rising. "Well, Mr. Satan, take a look around! What do you see? And to think we are meant to be the good guys, a tree freak, devil boy, and me, the freaky vampire elf! No wonder she's a little bit afraid!"

"Try and calm her down or something. I can't take that noise," Lucifer said, holding his hands over his ears. "She's worse than a fucking banshee, and I should know, I created them!"

Obsidian placed her hand on the girl's bloody, torn- up shoulder. She could see right down to the bone.

"Um, look… don't be afraid,. I'm not going to harm you, er … any more. What's your name?" She tried her best to sound calm, and caring.

Then looking down at her shoulder, Obsidian noticed that the girl's skin was staring to heal. She lifted her hand and saw that her shoulder almost looked normal again. She couldn't see the bones underneath anymore, and the skin had pulled itself back together. Shocked but also very relived, she put her other hand on the girl's leg. This was one of the many areas of her body that was a bloody, mangled mess.

"What's your name?" she asked again in the softest tone she could manage while her fangs were still partially extended.

"You're healing me? I feel all warm and tingly" the girl responded, while trying to move her limbs again.

"How sweet, the healing power of the elves lives on!" Lucifer skipped and danced around the room.
"it's just delightful."

"I'm Lucy." The girl finally answered Obsidian's question, she was now almost fully healed.

"Well, that's lovely Lucy. Now run along play times over" Lucifer was now standing by her side.

"*RUNNNNNNNNNNN!*" He screamed in her ear.

Lucy scrambled to her feet, and as fast as any human could, she fled from the room.

"Oops, she left her bra" Rowena was now back in her human form holding the remnants of Lucy's underwear in her hands. "Don't even ask." She shot a glance a Obsidian, who was not looking at all impressed by the situation.

I Have a Plan

Obsidian shook her head. She still wasn't feeling able to process what had just happened. First of all, finding her father, then, feeding on a human for the first time ever. Let alone all the stuff before that.

"I need to shower, get dressed, and when I come back I have a plan I'd like to talk through with you both," she informed Rowena and Lucifer. "I suggest you at least get dressed. Both of you!"

Around thirty minutes later, clean and clothed, Obsidian returned to the living room. Rowena was dressed and sitting on the sofa. Lucifer was also dressed and was gazing out the window.

"Well?" Obsidian decided to eventually chip away at the silence that seem to fill the room. A room that just under an hour ago was anything but silent.

"Hmm, well what?" Rowena yawned.

Lucifer didn't move, didn't stir, didn't even bother to move his head around. "Go on," he muttered, seeming disinterested.

"Well, my plan is, not that any of you care, by the way, and yes, I did come up with something useful, so stop acting like I just caught you at it or something OK?, You're both being really weird. Anyway, my point is, oh my god! Could one of you at least look at me when I'm talking here?!"

Rowena lifted her head. She looked like shame itself. "What did I just do? More to the point, what did we just do?" She sounded almost dazed.

"It's called fun, honey!" Lucifer spat, sounding like a spoilt child who had just been caught stealing the keys to his parents' car, "but Little Miss Prissy Pants had to go and spoil it."

"Look, I'm sorry, OK? But dial- a- date disasters aside, can we think about something a little more important here? My plan is as follows. Well when I saw my, ummm father, he was, well, doing something, well, someone in an alleyway, and he called her Lucy. Just like that other girl just called herself. She didn't look nice enough to be a Lucy, and my point is. well, Lucifer, you can look like anyone you want to anyone, if that makes sense. So if we track down, well, you know, and you look like Lucy, the real Lucy that is, my mother, well, I'm assuming so anyway. You could give him a message, like meet me in our field. Then when he goes there looking for her, we catch him off guard, and I don't know, attack him or something? Well, what do you think?" she asked suddenly feeling less sure about the whole situation.

Lucifer was looking thoughtful.

"Well, well, well. Hmm, brilliant, except I don't think my charm will work on him, unless he is already well engaged in activities with another woman. Then I could possibly give it a try. Wait, though, how did you know about the field?" His mocking tone turned to one of pure shock and intrigue.

"Oh mum, talks in her sleep. I heard her say something once like 'oh my darling, meet me in the field at noon, and I'll be ready,' or ew, you know what? I don't want to think about what she was thinking about. But it's the only time she ever talks," Obsidian said, like it was the most normal thing in the world.

"Sounds like I should pay your mother a visit!" Lucifer smiled, a very naughty looking smile.

"Oh no, you don't, you stay away from her," Obsidian shot back, feeling very protective of her mother.

"Children, please!" Rowena was now standing between Obsidian and Lucifer with both palms up, gesturing them to back down. They did. Obsidian stormed off to her room. Lucifer left. Rowena decided she needed a drink, but then thought better of it as she knew alcohol and blood didn't mix, and the last time she'd gone out for a cure for that she'd ended up in bed with the devil. So this time she took the safe option, and went to bed with herself.

Obsidian went to bed by herself too, but she wasn't alone for long. Lucifer decided to pay her a little visit. However after the antics of the evening gone by, she really just was not in the mood. So in her ever-so-polite manner, she told him to get stuffed.

Elf and Safety

After all the craziness, plotting, and scheming of the night before, the two girls were understandably a tad worse for wear. Rowena, however, believed she had just the thing to cure Obsidian's newfound taste for blood. Not another trip to an apothecary. She had learned her lesson. This was instead something altogether more wholesome that she had planned. It was a long overdue trip to the wooded side of town. To a place where they would find the last of the elves.

The elves hung out in secret, far away from the humans, and vampires of the city, for they would clearly stand out among the crowd. Unlike vampires, who had the whole druggy dropout look going for them, the elves looked like nothing on Earth. I'll spare you the story of how they are not from Earth, as Gaia has already filled you in on all that.

These elves were unfortunately on their last legs, so to speak. They had passed into the autumn stage of their incredibly long lives, and were reaching the winter fast. They had long burnt orange, and singed red hair. Their eyes matched the colour of their hair, and like their hair they were turning brown at the edges. Like the leaves on a dying tree, they were close to falling, getting caught up in a chilling breeze, and then being blown away. It was only a matter of time before they were gone. So Rowena had to take Obsidian to see them soon, before it was too late.

There were many theories about what happened to elves once they passed through the winter phase of their existence. One was that they became stars, even thought their bodies perished their souls would live on. They would go into the night sky, and shine on forevermore. They would start as shooting stars, flying through the sky until they found a place where they felt happy to spend an eternity. Another was that their souls were recycled and put into new elves, allowing their experience and knowledge to travel with them, meaning that the elves would get wiser with each new body. Either way it's not really important to this story.

When Obsidian finally surfaced and showered, it was past midday. Rowena had been up bright and early, and was getting annoyed with waiting for Obsidian as she tried to find something to wear. She settled on jeans and a black vest top. She found out her high black shoes from the club night, and decided she was ready to take on the world. She did a high kick and forced open her bedroom door. After, she checked the heel on her shoe, breathing a sigh of relief she was glad to see it wasn't broken.

"Pow! I'm ready for the world!" Obsidian burst her way into the living room.

"Well," said Rowena, ushering her out the door, "we are off to see a side of you, the nice side. The elf side. That's right, elf girl, we are gonna hang with the woodland folk, the last of the elves on Earth, that ain't your grand folk, at least."

"Wait, though, what about my shoes? And wait, you said grand folk? It's just my grandma that's knocking around these days. What really happened to my granddad?" Obsidian tried to halt Rowena, and stall her but her attempts were futile. She was at the top of the stairs in no time, and out the main door before Rowena spoke again.

"We can talk and walk, yeah? Just follow me and listen. You can do that, right? Good. Well, your grandparents are among the highest, most powerful elves going, and when your granddad found out that your mum was having you, he flipped his top, and went mental. He was not a happy bunny. He went up to the main Man and wanted him to put a stop to it. But the Man wouldn't let him, and kept him up there so he wouldn't ruin things. He saw the bigger picture. Or so I was lead to believe." Rowena was giving Obsidian the short, tamed down version of events. Now wasn't the time for getting into Obsidian's family history. Rowena wanted her to have a clear head, and leave with a positive image of the elves.

They passed the rest of the walk in silence, Obsidian was too busy checking on her shoes to make any real attempts at a conversation. They were off roading it big style, heading through the park, and out of the city. Soon, walking at their super quick pace, (even in heels Obsidian could walk faster than you or I could run), they reached the fields. They had left the city centre far behind, and were heading to a large cluster of trees. A wood. Not like the forest where Obsidian used to live, but a wood that was just as magical nonetheless.

The elves had been waiting a long time for Obsidian to visit them. They wanted to know all about the one who was taking over on their task of protecting the humans. They wanted to know how one soul could match the power of many. It had drained so much of their power to do this task, cutting their lives short. How could one single person have any hope of making a dent in the vampire epidemic?. Their wait was finally over, they were about to see Obsidian in all her, um, glory.

Fed up, and splattered head to toe in mud, Obsidian walked into the wood and into the home of the elves. They were sitting in a clearing huddled around a fire. There was a large, wooden shed like building to the left of the clearing. This was where the elves lived. There were only four left now. They had a small vegetable patch next to the shed, and they lived off this and the things that the wood provided. Mushrooms, nuts, berries, and bunnies. Yeah, that's right, cute little bunnies. They had already eaten when the two arrived, and left nothing to share.

They were not impressed with what they saw. The saviour of the human race, in a muddy vest top. Her jeans plastered in mud, and her shoes where caked in it, so much so they couldn't see her feet. One elf spoke, it was a female whose hair was getting really brown. She was old. Really old.

"So, you are what we have been waiting all these years for, the one to save the human race. I see." That was all she said; the others just stared at Obsidian.

"Um, yes, because you have done such an amazing job yourselves," Obsidian retorted. "I mean, check you out, living in a shed in the woods. Hiding away while that city out there and fuck knows where else is getting turned into a vampire's playground. I don't know why I dragged my ass across that shit pit to get here, or why Rowena thinks you're so great. But I don't see anything here that is meant to inspire me to embrace my elf side. OK, so vampires are not so great either, but why can't I just be me, a weird combination of the two? Me, a mix of the two best and strongest elves and vampires. I guess that's why I am the ONE that can solve all this mess. You have clearly spent far too long here. Maybe it's time you left. Cleared off. If you really want to help, give me your power, and go. We don't need you. I don't need you and your condescending looks. You are free to leave. Class dismissed!"

Her rant was truly inspiring to the elves. She showed that she had true spirit, and that maybe she was right. More than that, maybe she was ready to take over.

Then something happened. It was something no one was expecting, and not even the elves had planned. They were tired, and they were fed up with expending their power to perform this futile task. They wanted out. They knew this now. So they stood up and formed a circle. Joining hands, they forced their powers into a large ball. A large blue ball of power. For a second two of them let go of each other's hands, breaking the circle. One of the elves. The one who spoke waved her free hand at the ball of power. It surged toward her, then when it was in her hand she turned and threw it at Obsidian.

The ball surrounded her then imploded and penetrated her. Rushing straight to her heart. It mixed with her own power, and her violet light shone even brighter. Her eyes became more vivid, an outlet for her power. The elves faded, flickered, then vanished.

Rowena was for the first time in a long time totally shocked, and totally stunned for words. This wasn't what she had planned either. Maybe a nice chat, talk about elfy stuff to show how they lived off the land, not off humans. Although on this front Rowena was a bit of a hypocrite. *But hey I cant help it im a tree. Or so she told herself.* She looked at Obsidian, whose eyes were blazing with all this new power and strength. This had gone better, oh so much better than she could have planned.

Something was happening to Obsidian, though; her eyelids flickered and her eyes rolled. She was having a power rush. Rowena was at her side before she fainted. She would need rest, a chance to adjust, and get use to all this new strength. Time that they just didn't have. Rowena scoped up Obsidian, and ran as fast as she could back to their flat.

With Obsidian safely tucked up in bed, Rowena decided she needed a much deserved drink or two. She raided her alcohol cabinet and poured herself a large glass of white rum, added a splash of lemonade and a twist of lime, and threw in a straw. With that she made her way to her own bedroom. She was exhausted from having to run for miles at breakneck speed carrying Obsidian, who was much heavier than her slight frame suggested. Rowena crawled into her bed and took a big sip of her drink. She was going to sleep well tonight.

Lets Do This Shit

The next day Lucifer was up bright and early so was Obsidian. After her slightly rude awakening, what with Lucifer poking her and saying, "Wake up, sleepy bum," she decided it was time to put her plan from the other night into action.

"Well maybe you *should* go see my mum, I mean, if she is really in the field, then it really will catch him off guard. Just please promise me you won't try anything! With her," she begged, putting her new powers to the test. She could do without Lucifer hooking up with her mother.

"Oh, come on, if she's as hot as the rumours say she is, I wont be able to resist!" Lucifer jested.

"Well, I don't know; she is my mum, but she looks even weirder than I do, and I swear she used to have green eyes and …,"

"Green eyes are hot!"

"And green hair!" Obsidian shouted back, annoyed at having been interrupted

"Oh, not so hot. What's she like now?" Lucifer was having fun winding Obsidian up, she was such an easy target he just couldn't resist. Plus he found her 'cute' when she was annoyed.

"UHH you know what? Go see for yourself!" She gave up, new powers or not. What would be, would be.

And Lucifer didn't hang around either. He had succeeded in getting Obsidian really wound up, but couldn't resist he urge to go and see her mum. He needed to see her anyway, otherwise the plan they had wouldn't work. It didn't take him long to get to the forest, or to sweet talk his way in. Once he'd used his powers of persuasion on some very tough looking minotaurs, he rushed straight to Lucy's room. She was still fast asleep and sleep talking, among other things. When Lucifer woke up the very aroused Lucy, he realised that Obsidian was right, she did look weird. Her hair was boring, her eyes were boring. All brown! No fire, no flames, no hints of green. All just plain old boring brown! Maybe the whole thing about elves changing like the seasons was true, Lucifer sighed. Would her true love still love her now that she had changed from a beautiful autumn leaf to a dead winter one? He said his piece quickly while Lucy was still half asleep and convinced she was talking to the vampire, and then left.

"I came, I saw, and I went, and yeah, old mother dear, oh dear, what happens to you elf ladies? You go all drab like a wilted rose. You can see it was a perfect bloom once, then it goes all brown around the edges." He sighed.

"Is that a problem for you?" Obsidian asked bluntly, sounding angry. She was also shocked at how quickly he had made it back. It was like he had never left. Above everything else she was curious to know what had happened to her mother's powers, and why she faded to brown so young. Obsidian was surging with power, and decided she wanted to put it all to the test.

Lucifer brought Obsidian back to the real trouble at hand, before she really had a chance to unleash all the pent up power she held inside. "It could be a problem if Daddy dear doesn't recognise Mummy elf."

With that comment Rowena emerged from the bathroom.

"Well, only one way to find out. Let's go see him" She was wearing a see through cream lace dress, and the dial- a-whore's red underwear, well, what was left of it.

"What? I washed them, by hand. They're delicate, and designer. When I'm done killing vampires, I'm gonna start fucking them. There is clearly more money in that!" she laughed. Although she was partly serious. Rowena didn't do jokes, not really.

"That's if there are any left to fuck after Daddy dear goes back to hell." That was another thing Obsidian managed to say in the casual tone she had now perfected.

Lucifer spoke up his words were full of angry venom.. "Honey, there will be, I mean, where they all gonna go? Most of their souls are already in hell, they ain't gonna stop putting on a show the second the master puppeteer leaves town. They're not like Pinocchio, they're all real boys and girls. Just cuz they are looking for a soul to replace theirs doesn't mean they don't still have their minds. I'm fed up with people thinking they are mindless, blood sucking, soul stealing zombies! that are all gonna die the second their master heads to hell! They can't die unless he does, and he can't die on Earth, you need to kill him in hell. When the last drop of all his victims' blood leaves his body, the ones he turned will die. When they die, the ones they turned die, too, and so on. Its like dominoes,"

"How can you be so sure?" both Rowena and Obsidian asked in unison.

"Because I fucking created them that way. I needed a back up plan, in case things went wrong. Wanna know how he got out?, well, I let him out! That's right I did it, it's all my fault! I thought I could stop him, turns out I can't. I can't kill my own creations or fucking control them! One night! One fucking night, that's all I allowed him, but he went fucking AWOL! On my fucking ass!" He was really mad now.

"OK, now calm down, and breathe," soothed Rowena. "I'm the only one allowed the freak outs around here, OK? I'm Miss Meltdown, remember? Yeah, I heard, I have ears. We need you to make this work, and it won't work if you don't! You let out an evil vampire, who wouldn't get back into his box, so what? You're the devil or whatever, you're evil, you do your own thing, you don't listen to rules, you set them or break them. I bet you only did it to piss off the Almighty, that's why I killed a few innocent people cuz he can't, and I knew that would piss him off. It's fun, we all need fun, even Obsidian over there needs fun. So what do you say? we hit the town, find our Pinocchio and put his strings back on?"

Rowena had given her best shot at giving a pep talk to a now distraught Lucifer. She hoped for all their sakes it was enough.

No Strings Attached

Back on track and back in the mood to flirt (even if it was with a man), Lucifer decided to go looking for his puppet, or poppet, as he was thinking of calling him. So he took off with Rowena, who was now dressed in a figure hugging electric blue dress. The colour complimented her tanned skin tone perfectly. They searched the city streets for any signs of the vampire, annoyed that he could move as freely, and quickly in daylight as he could at nighttime. Unlike the other vampires who were faster at night, as the cold light of the moon seemed to energise them. The sun, on the other hand, seemed to make them seem slow and lethargic.

They decided to split up, giving them a better chance of finding him faster. When one of them found him, they would send a message to the other using their minds. As they could both move fast, they could quickly navigate their way to the other's location. Lucifer gave up on all the usual vamp hangouts and quickly made his way to the notorious red light zone. It wasn't only called a red light zone by those with the ability to see the red power emitted by the vampires. In the later years the few humans that lived there often had red lights in their houses.

Lucifer stopped in his tracks, and shivered, which was unlike him. What he'd witnessed he found very disturbing. Disturbing even for him. A girl with Coca Cola hair and violet eyes who wasn't Obsidian! It was the dial- a-whore girl. *Bitch!* He thought, *stealing my girl's look.* And she wasn't alone; she was summoning a man, a man Lucifer knew all to well, and this was one messed up scene he didn't want to see played out.

Just then Rowena turned up. "Should have known I'd find you in the red light district. It's ironic, really, that humans can't see the red lights these fuckers give out and put up their own ones that they can see. And oh my, is that the wench from the other night?"

"The one whose bra and panties you're wearing? Yes, it is" Lucifer said with a wink and a smile.

"Who's the guy, and ooh, oh my god, this is wrong. You need to go over there right now and stop them" Rowena was shocked when she realised who the man was.

"What, as myself or as Mother dear?" Lucifer's sick sense of humour was starting to surface.

"Ew! Um, I don't know, Lucy, I guess. And can they hear us? I mean, they are just across from us" Rowena gestured at the distance between them.

They were behind an old warehouse, and Lucifer and Rowena could see Obsidian's father and the dial-a-whore across the car park.

"We can't tell Obsidian about this this, agreed? Right, Lucifer?"

But Lucifer was already making his way across the car park. He planted himself in between the girl and, um, *him*, and smiled. She ran away screaming. Thoughts of the night before flooded through her mind.

"Perfect, just you and me. I can't stop thinking about you, and me and our field. Meet me there tonight!" Lucifer swooned while planting images of Lucy, the real Lucy, into the vampire's mind. Deep down he knew he could find a way to make the plan work. He would do it for Obsidian. He hated himself for having feelings for her, if you could call them that, and he had unfinished business with another that he still need to fix. He was

Satan, for god's sake. He didn't have feelings. Least of all for girls.

With that, Lucifer was off. Rowena caught a glimpse of a girl dressed as a witch fleeing the scene. She smiled; the plan was working.

The vampire was pacing. He was thinking, *"Lucy?"* but there was only one way to find out, and that wouldn't happen until later. He fled the scene, too.

So that's how he saw Lucy, as a witch, not an elf at all. *Oh shit,* thought Rowena, unsure how she was able to see what he saw. It troubled her, though. Lucy wasn't a witch. She didn't even look like one. Rowena knew all too well how bland and normal Lucy looked now, just like a regular human. But she pushed her doubts to the side. They had to make this work. She just needed to work out how. She decided to regroup with the others, and formulate a new plan.

Rowena found Lucifer and Obsidian back at the flat.

"Tonight?" Obsidian screeched. "As in *tonight*? As in"

"Yes, tonight!" Lucifer yelled back

"What time? Did you at least specify a time?" Obsidian was getting annoyed now.

"Yeah, night time." Lucifer matched her tone.

"OK, guys! Could you save all the pent- up, um, anger for tonight? Maybe?" Rowena's request fell on deaf ears. Full of anger, Obsidian left the room.

Rowena sighed and turned to Lucifer. "Um, don't we have a problem? He sees Lucy as a witch. I caught a glimpse of a witch running away when we saw, well, you know. I don't know how I saw you as that, but I did. And well as we both know Lucy is far from witchlike. She looks drab and, well, human! You never know; hopefully she still has the outfit. But she doesn't have her elf like glow anymore. It's like she's given up, and lost all her power. I've watched her over the years. She has gotten more and more like a human like. Using, her powers up as fast as she can. I don't understand how or why." Rowena seemed unusually concerned.

Lucifer patted her on the shoulder. "Oh, Row, don't worry. I'll intervene if I have to. Now run along and get ready. I'll have it all under control."

Rowena left feeling slightly happier about the situation. The only one not convinced was Lucifer himself. *Will he see through me, or will my charms work on him a second time? Ew.* He shuddered. *I could just project the images of Lucy into his mind again, and hope it's enough.* He hated that he wasn't sure, and that he'd created something a plan that was as good as it was. It had to have a fault. Whatever it was, Lucifer was sure he was too blinded by his own arrogance to see it.

Tonight's the Night

After Rowena had slipped in to something a little more appropriate for vampire slaying/ sending back to hell, she decided to pop into Obsidian's room to see how she was doing. It wasn't good. Obsidian wasn't there. There was no note no nothing.

"Great, she's gone and left me to do it all myself. Brilliant. I always knew she was fucking useless… and" She paused, sensing someone else in the room.

"Uh- hm," the voice responded

"Hello! Who's there?" Rowena asked, trying not to sound scared.

"Oh, Missy No Faith, it's your fairy fucking god-mother!" The voice spoke again. Then in a puff of pink smoke, the body behind the voice appeared.

"Oh, Luce, it's you." Rowena wasn't sure why she was disappointed to see Lucifer, after all, his pink fairy outfit and glittery wings were amusing, even if they left little to the imagination. She blinked and shook her head, he really was dressed as a fairy!

"What, you've never seen a man in pink before?!" He said disbelievingly.

"Um, well, erh, what's the occasion?" She was unsure where this was leading.

"I stole a few flying horses and a carriage from the fucked up forest, thought it would be nice to travel in style. Plus Sid stole your car!" he said nonchalantly

"What? When? She can't even drive!" Rowena really was scared now.

"You were de-whoring yourself in the shower all afternoon, so Obsidian decided she couldn't wait, and OK, I'm a crap liar; I drove her in your car, but still it was her idea! She was restless and getting all cranky and stuff. So I took her to the field. I also found the lovely winged specimens I have waiting outside, and well, here I am!" He'd lied about the last part. Winged horses are not just left hanging around on street corners.

Rowena noticed the lights flickering by the window, and realised he wasn't lying. The flickering was caused by the flapping of wings! Big, white wings! Attached to a big white Pegasus! Well, there where two, and a big fairy princess carriage! She could think of a thousand things to say, and reasons why it was a bad idea. They'd be seen, for one. But not one of these reasons was enough to stop her from getting into that ridiculous carriage. She wasn't allowed to ride the horses when they were in the forest. Gaia wouldn't let her. They weren't normal horses, you can't just ride a Pegasus. Well, technically she wouldn't be riding it.

She'd forgotten everything, the second she stepped out of the window and into the carriage. Her swords, bows arrows, her ability to think straight. Let alone how to fight. She was immersed in soft, white, luxurious fabrics, softer than velvet, smoother than silk. Fresher, than the finest Egyptian cotton. She was in an enormous bed! Bigger than the carriage itself. The air smelt dreamy, like lemons and Turkish delight and cherries. Mmm, she could taste cherries, and there it was among the sheets and sheets of luxury she found her favourite thing ever. Cherry wine. Her own bottle. She drank it without thinking twice. She didn't have time to think once, she was out. Fast asleep and dreaming.

Meanwhile Obsidian was sat freezing her ass off in a field. She jumped up when she saw Lucifer. He had insisted on taking the car back, but now arrived on foot. "I couldn't find her! I looked everywhere, shops, bars, ex-boyfriends' beds, well, you know, and nothing, she's cleaned out, left town. Gone!" He was lying again, and was finding that he was loving it. He was starting to feel like himself again. He smiled, then cleared his expression. He had to at least act the part of being concerned.

"Did you check the parks and the alleyways and…, I mean, did you look everywhere!?" Obsidian was panicking. She needed Rowena here, now with her. She couldn't fight him her father on her own. After the first time she saw him, She wasn't sure she could fight him at all. She wasn't sure of anything right now, and the fact that Rowena had abandoned her in her time of need showed she had no faith in her. She really was fucked.

Lucifer nodded. "Yep, everywhere! Turns out she's all talk and no action. Maybe the warrior princess, is more princess than warrior." He spun around round to face Obsidian, she. She was sat sitting with her head in her hands, rocking back and forth. Unbeknown to her Lucifer had set the whole thing up, so that he could show Obsidian that maybe she really was capable of doing something herself. After all it was her plan, Rowena would only step in at the wrong moment and try and undermine Obsidian. She was always doing that, and besides with what he had planed for her there was no place for Rowena to be by her side.

"Ahhhhhhhhhhhhhhhhhhhhhhhhhhhhhhhhhh! I can't do this." She was starting to cry. which was odd she never cried. Was she really ready to let down her guard? Well even if she was this wasn't really the time or the place for it. As things had started to happen, and happen fast. For the plan to work they needed to get moving. Her mother had just arrived in the field, and Obsidian needed to focus "Shit, mum!" She jumped up back on her feet and pointed up the field. She did not approve of her mothers choice of outfit. Lucifer grabbed her and rushed across the field, where they hid like a children behind a tree. He couldn't risk being seen, as it would ruin everything. Lucy, and the vampire had to believe they were the only two people in the field. That it was fate bringing them back together, and not some sinister plan destroy him.

The leaves on the trees began to stir, but the air was still. Even Lucifer and Obsidian were still. She was witnessing the first time she had ever seen her parents together.

One tepee appeared in the middle of the field, a flag wavered on the top and the front flaps blew open. There *he* was standing in front of the tepee, glass in hand, gazing at her.

"You're so, um, so..." He paused trying to find the right words.

"Plain!" Lucifer whispered more to himself than anyone else. She wasn't even wearing the witch costume. Instead she had opted for a baby blue camisole, and knee high boots Damn it. How stupid was she?

"Shh!" Obsidian hit him on the arm. She'd heard him. He'd forgotten about her amazing senses. Besides her brown hair Obsidian had never seen her mother look less plain in all her life

"Kiss me!" Lucy demanded.

"Gross! Look away now!" This time Lucifer whispered it in Obsidian's ear. But she couldn't look away. She wasn't looking at her, um, parents making out, she was looking at the black glass in *his* hand.

"What's with the glass? I mean, it's not really glass! Though, surely?" she asked, seriously wanting an answer.

"No, it's a goblet, and the bastard he stole my favourite one. I got the dragon one back, but he stole my pure obsidian one, too." Lucifer spat, out annoyed by how much the vampire had tricked him. He would pay for this. Lucifer would make sure of it.

"Obsidian!?" Obsidian asked, checking that she'd heard right.

"Yes, you're named after the one thing in hell that can kill vampires. Unfortunately, my new name for the Under World, or realm for the dead wicked or wicked dead, never took off, Obsidian. I had one goblet made out of it, he must have taken it the night I let him go." Lucifer tried to keep a lid on his anger. Now wasn't the time to lose control.

"But why obsidian!" She was really asking two questions.

"Sadly I don't, well, didn't have trees down there, no need for them, you see. No one breathes when they're dead!" Lucifer was losing his cool, quickly. He wasn't in the mood for Obsidian's stupid questions.

"But why obsidian!" She hadn't quite gotten the answer she was looking for.

"It's black and dark and beautiful." Once more Lucifer wasn't talking to anyone, just himself.

"But why am *I* called Obsidian?" Obsidian hit his arm to get his attention.

"It's the only thing that can kill vampires, idiot!" He stepped out from behind the tree, almost in a trance. Obsidian tried to get ahold of him and pull him back, but it was too late. He stepped on a twig, a large twig. The sound of the snap could have woken the dead. It certainly stirred the undead. He was making his way straight towards her parents.

Obsidian ran after him to try to stop him, whatever he was playing at, he could ruin everything. Little did she know he was trying to help out, to make this bad situation better. What Obsidian couldn't see is that Lucifer now resembled the image of Lucy as a witch. The vampire was starting to think this Lucy was just another fake, another girl who had heard of his Lucy obsession. He was confused, which one if any was the real Lucy. Lucifer could read his mind, and needed to convince him that he really was the real Lucy. However Obsidian, had messed up that plan, if only she had used her new, enhanced power, and read Lucifer's mind, she would have thought twice before she took any action. For she was now standing next to Lucifer, and was facing her father, and her mother. She wanted not only to stop Lucifer, she also wanted to get the glass if she had that then she could have ended the vampire once and for all. The glass now unfortunately lay smashed on the ground. He The vampire had dropped it the second he realised one of the Lucy's was Lucifer. When he saw Lucifer as himself, the evil demon that created him, he knew it was a trap. Not knowing what the glass was, he broke it. Not his best plan to date.

Obsidian never made it to the shards of obsidian now strewn on the ground. A white carriage drawn by two white Pegasus caught her attention. Rowena was still fast asleep inside. Obsidian, was slightly confused by the entrance of the carriage. She knew it, of course, it was Gaia's personal carriage. Grandmother had caught her playing in it once, and warned her to stay away from it. She was unsure why Gaia would need it to travel such a small distance, or why she was there at all. When no one stepped out of the elaborate carriage, Obsidian sensed something was really wrong. She ran over to it and stepped up inside the carriage. Inside she found Rowena, she shook Rowena, but she didn't stir. Unsure why Obsidian checked for a pulse, did Rowena even have a pulse? She did, it was faint, but somehow something caused the fluid to stir and flow in her veins. Did she have a heart? The question went unanswered, for Rowena didn't wake up.

"Shit, well, I hope I don't need you," muttered Obsidian holding Rowena's hand. She wanted to fly away, far away. But where could she go? After all she was needed here. She had a big mess to sort out.

When You're Gone

Obsidian heard a sound in the distance, getting closer by the second. It was the sound of giant wings flapping. She jumped out of the carriage just in time; the sight of the dragon startled the Pegasus', and they took flight again. Bright pink flames blazing Torch headed straight to the vampire. She had sensed that Obsidian was in danger and had flown as fast as she could from the Isle of Dragons. The other dragons had tried to stop her, saying she couldn't abandon the Tree, but Torch disobeyed them all giving up her post. She knew it was never really the job for her. She was Obsidian's guardian, and she should have never left her. She was here now, jaws wide open and teeth as sharp blades and as strong as diamonds she descended on *him*. She assessed the situation, and he needed to be removed from it. He was dangerous, not just to Obsidian, but to everyone. Even Lucy wasn't safe. When she was close enough she let out an almighty roar. In a blaze of pink flames and a flash of diamond white teeth he was gone.

Torch let out another jet of flames and a different sounding roar. A sound of pain shout out of her. She fell to the ground. Red hot pink lava flowed from her. Anger rumbled inside her. She turned her head to face her attacker. Obsidian was at her side, and made her way around Torch. She too wanted to face the attacker. Obsidian was just in time to see her mother with a shard of the broken goblet in her hand. Seconds later she screamed as Torch let out one final jet of flame. Obsidian was sure she saw a hand come out of the ground and pull her mother down. It pulled her down as she was engulfed in flames.

"Ahhhhhhhhhhhhhhhhhhhhhhhhhhhhhhhhhhhhhh hhhhhhhhhhhhhhhh!" Obsidian let out a long scream and fell to her feet. She noticed something then, blood on the ground. Not the burning pink lava that flowed through Torch, but the dark red kind that ran through the veins of humans. She looked at her wrists, she had never seen her own blood shed before. Was it the same as human blood? she wondered. Was it the same as her mother's? A hand on her shoulder brought her back to her senses. It was Lucifer.

"I see she made the sacrifice then" He cast a glance at the blood on the ground.

"How do you mean?" Obsidian was puzzled it had all happened so quickly. It was a blur even in her mind.

"To make the passage to the realm of the wicked dead, that's my new name for it. If you'd listened earlier you would have known that anyway a pure soul must make the ultimate sacrifice, and take its own life. I guess it works for elves too" He shrugged his shoulders and turned away.

"She was burning!" Obsidian cried out.

"She would have died a pure soul, and returned to the higher realm unhurt, but she chose to follow her heart, the silly bitch" was Lucifer's answer.

"The hand? I... .. I saw a hand?" It was starting to sink in, and the cogs in Obsidian's mind worked overtime to process everything that had just taken place.

"Oh, the hand of the soul grabber. He grabs the souls of the pure and drags them down when they shed their own lives" Lucifer was looking at Torch now. "Shame about your dragon, I could have done with one like that" With that he was gone.

Obsidian blinked her eyelashes heavy with tears she didn't even know she cried.

"Obsidian!!!!!!!!!!!!!!!" a voice called out.

"Rowena?" This came out as a question that she seemed only to ask herself.-Although she already knew the answer. Standing in the middle of the field were Rowena, and Gaia. Obsidian used the last of her energy to run to them. She hugged Rowena, who stood awkwardly, unsure of what to do. It was Gaia who spoke.

"Well this I did not see. Torch sacrificed herself for you, and I thought she was going to stay on Dragon Isle. Alas she sensed you were in danger and returned; her bond with you was strong and cost her dearly. My poor child born of clay and flames."

Without seeming to walk, Gaia appeared next to Torch. She placed her hand on the now great albeit dead dragon and muttered a few inaudible words. In front of both Rowena's and Obsidian's eyes, Torch was no longer a dragon she had become a hill. A large hill covered in lush emerald green grass, shaped like a sleeping dragon. Gaia turned and glanced at the girls; then in a flash of lightning and a gust of wind she was gone.

"Hmm…yeah so where the hell have you been? You missed it all?" Obsidian asked Rowena while still staring at the hill that was once her guardian dragon.

"Sleeping," Rowena admitted. "Lucifer tricked me, but it doesn't look like you needed me anyway, so I guess no harm done right? Well, not to you anyway. I'm not sure how I ended up here, though, but I'm glad I did"

"Ooh, I guess in an odd way things did kinda work out here, so what are we going to do now?" a slightly-lost-feeling Obsidian asked.

"I don't know about you, but I've still got vampires to kill!" Rowena replied with a smile on her face.

"Oh right yeah so I guess Lucifer was right, damn him! And the vampires will only all die when their master does, and as he is from hell he needs to die there Great!" Obsidian knew what was coming, and she didn't like it. Not one tiny little bit. She glanced down at her wrist and shivered.

"Sorry hun I can't help you there. I'm stuck here so you'll have to go it alone" Rowena seemed a little pissed off by this fact.

"Except she won't be alone she will have me" Lucifer was back looking as devilishly handsome as ever. He held out his hand to Obsidian "Can't have you spilling your blood too, now can we, so thought I'd give you my hand to hell. So to speak"

She took it and was gone, dragged down to a place that she could never imagine, a place so different to the forest she had known all her life. But was it different from the place she knew now? She would have to find out. All she knew as she was ripped from the world and pulled painfully down in to the depths of the unknown was that she was leaving Rowena alone to hunt vampires. I'm sure Rowena didn't mind though.